A TOUCH OF THE OTHER

A TOUCH OF THE OTHER

by

CLARE MORGAN

LONDON
VICTOR GOLLANCZ LTD
1983

Published in association with Arrow Books

British Library Cataloguing in Publication Data
Morgan, Clare
  A touch of the other.
  I. Title
  823'.914[F]   PR6063.0/

  ISBN 0-575-03284-7

Photoset in Great Britain by
Rowland Phototypesetting Limited, Bury St Edmunds, Suffolk
and printed by St Edmundsbury Press
Bury St Edmunds, Suffolk

For Coed and the shadow of Cader;
for Enge; and for Anne.

I

It was three o'clock. Wankel was walking down Lazarus Street rehearsing how he would tell Suzie he loved her. He did not love her; but he had known her for three days now, and he felt the time for action had arrived; and besides, past experience had taught him that saying you loved them was a strategy which worked.

He paused briefly in his thinking about love and Suzie as the hour struck close above his head in the belfry of St Lazarus' church. Three o'clock; his whole life seemed to be composed of threes: three wives; three children; three days; Suzie was thirty-three. He cast round in his mind to see if anything else would fit and noticed, with a sense of something like alarm, that he was passing the wet fish shop, Number 300 Lazarus Street. He crossed himself surreptitiously, afraid for the moment that there might be as much in it as he liked to pretend. Then he dropped his hand back to his side and put it in his pocket, hoping no one had seen. He was not a religious man, but he did believe, in a patchy, on-off kind of way, in a retributive God; and the church clock's chimes were echoing sonorously through his brain.

Not that he had cause for guilt. God could strip his soul at any time, pick it clean. There was nothing Wankel needed to hide; or nothing much. He was a normal man with normal weaknesses; but God was a man too, and would surely be tolerant of those.

He scowled and buttoned his overcoat more tightly round his throat. It was a sign of nervousness. Into his mind came not the reassuring image of God as one of the boys, but as a great vulture, picking him clean, tearing strips of flesh and sinew from white bone, his bone. He swallowed the beginnings of a scream

7

and looked round him uneasily; it seemed so real. How would he explain it at the hospital? 'A vulture attacked me in Lazarus Street': they'd lock him up. But it did seem real.

He found he had been holding his breath as if in anticipation of the great beak seizing him. He looked down to make sure he was still all there: the important pieces seemed to be intact. Reassured he breathed out slowly, enjoyably. My imagination, he thought, and smiled, but not too widely in case he showed his crooked tooth. My imagination! He thought it ruefully but with a pleasurable affection; his imagination was his single most important gift. For Wankel was a poet. Already his mind was busy working on that image of God as a vulture; about sixteen lines, hmm, that should do it; visual layout ragged, like the vulture's wings, rhythm staccato like the random stabbings of its beak. The first line came to him: 'As I was walking past the church'. No, no! He groaned, and caught at his bottom lip with his crooked tooth. 'The church clock chimed, a sonorous bell . . .' But all he could think of to follow it was 'The verger's drunk, and sick as hell'.

He shrugged and turned up his coat collar. It had begun to rain. He thought of getting out his notebook to write down his ideas for the poem. But the rain was slanting uncomfortably into his face, his hands would get wet, the book too. It could wait until he got home.

He thought about Suzie again and how he should approach her. How should it be? 'You know, Suzie, I do love you'. No, not subtle enough. How about 'I *might* love you'? What was he thinking of – that was almost an insult. Well then: 'I *could* love you'. Ah! That was it! Full of promise, empty of commitment, entirely seductive. 'I *could* love you'. That beautifully implied 'if'; it was guaranteed to set their minds like ferrets at a foxhole. If . . . what? If I wear my hair *so*? Wear *this* dress? Say B rather than A? It was a woman's weakest point, thought Wankel, this uncertainty about her lovableness. Wankel had no such uncertainty about himself. Women found him irresistible – oh, not for his looks – what was mere physical appearance? No, they wanted him for his mind.

8

But were there any on whom it would not work, who would not take the bait the 'if' implied, who would say 'take me as I am or not at all'? Wankel doubted it; and on the whole preferred things as they were. He did not want his pursuit of women to take up too much of the energy rightfully devoted to his Art.

His Art. 'My Art'. He mouthed the words, savouring them, their silent shape. He imagined how they would sound broadcast over the airwaves of Radio 4. 'Oh yes, I subordinate everything for the sake of my Art'. It did sound quite grand. Wives, children, bank managers – all as nothing compared to Art. 'Art is a continuum; my Art is but a speck on the now of that continuum, which owes its existence to the past and to the future'. Hmm. He liked that; he liked it very much. But he felt instinctively it would have more lasting impact in print. He decided he would save it. It would look well as a quote in a half-page *Guardian* profile; with a photograph of course, top right, head and shoulders. He made a conscious effort to lengthen his shortish neck. Head and shoulders: he would look noble, fine. Perhaps he should try the phrases out on Suzie.

Suzie. He took his thin hands out of his pockets and rubbed them together. That little wine bar, two doors from the Fighting Cock; the lighting dim, the music not too loud; a bottle of house red and a burned down candle between them. He would lean across the table, take her hand. . . .

As he turned out of Lazarus Street the rain increased, backed by a gusting wind which drove it even into the usually sheltered doorways. Wankel did not notice. He was imagining that top button of Suzie's which she never did do up, and how, as she bent towards him earnestly (too earnestly, if he were honest with himself) the vee of the material would open slightly and reveal the still strangely childish softness of the flesh of her chest. He sighed, a breathy sigh of pure lust. Suzie. She was a remarkable woman, for thirty-three. He began to hum, no more than a small vibration in the back of his throat.

*

About a mile from Lazarus Street, the houses begin to verge on to respectability. But between the straight-onto-the-street squalor which Wankel has passed through without thinking, and that life-goal, the suburban semi, lies the no-man's land of the Victorian Terrace. Here a battle is being fought. Here the buyers, young, hopeful and impecunious, must take their choice. Will the Terrace rise to the heady status of 'urban cottages', where house-guests squeeze themselves at weekends into inconvenient corners (*such* a lot of character, you know!) and fill the cloakroom with the dubious scents of half-digested garlic? Or will it fall into disrepair, to be blind-windowed with asbestos sheeting, abused by graffiti, pissed on by winos and vagrants?

In such a state of indecision rests the house where Wankel's Suzie lives. She is 'Wankel's Suzie' because it is through him that she has so far been defined. And because he hopes to follow up the possession of her image with the possession – however temporarily – of her Self. Or at least that most obvious of all the attributes of her self – her flesh, her blood, her body. How little has changed since George Eliot said, more than a hundred years ago, 'we do not ask what a woman is; we ask to whom she belongs'.

Suzie sat in her bedroom window, thinking of Wankel. The rain, beating up against the pane, disturbed her. She was easily disturbed; by noises, faces, her own thoughts. She had seen, printed on a postcard in a health food shop, the phrase 'considering how frightening life is, it is not very dangerous', and had been impressed by it. But it was not a view she shared. For Suzie, life was a dangerous and uncertain thing. Even such an action as getting up in the morning presented a hundred difficult decisions. Breathing itself was problematical: in-out, or out-in? Sometimes her husband, Lanky Larry, would say to her, 'What is it with you Suzie? What is it?' And she would stare at him round-eyed and dumb, like a half-snared rabbit, the same scream welling through her gut but unarticulated; stare at him, balding (why must all my men be balding?), fingering frustratedly at his flecked beard, he on one side, she on the other, but of what she was not sure.

And the addition to her life of the Poet had increased its danger and its complication. She thought of Wankel as 'the Poet' or more especially as 'my Poet'. For Suzie was a collector, she liked things to belong to her so that she felt she had control of them. She already owned a china pig with eyes rather like Wankel's; she saved small coins inside its darkened abdomen. 'My piggy-wiggy bank' she would croon sometimes, stroking it softly with the very ends of her fingers, as she had yesterday stroked Wankel's hand.

The rain disturbed her. She looked out of the window and saw a single raincoated figure struggling with an umbrella which the wind had turned inside out. She thought, what am I going to do with Wankel, almost sure that she did not know. The question had occupied her mind more or less exclusively since she had felt his thigh pressing into hers at the Free Lunchtime Organ Recital three days previously. What am I going to do with Wankel? Or the wider question – what *does* one do with a poet? She had never met a poet in the flesh before. Writers had always fascinated her; writing was so esoteric. She wrote a little herself, when she had time. She was a member of the Green Street Writers' Circle, and she treasured in her desk drawer a photograph of the youthful Dylan Thomas. But Wankel, she acknowledged, was different, a rarity among writers: he was neither unpublished nor dead.

Suzie was supposed to be writing now. She had been commissioned to write an article on *Wag-On*, her local Women's Action Group's newspaper. She had pasted a sticker to the glass panel of her green front door, facing outwards, which said 'WAG for Women'. Suzie believed in WAG and the Women's Movement; but somehow the thought of Wankel banished creativity from her brain. His image disturbed her. It provoked in her a queer combination of feelings: a sick twisting of the gut such as she felt before going to the dentist; and a pure physical tension as if her nerves and sinews had been pulled out one by one and stretched upon a rack. Wankel. She had filled up half a page with his name; half a page which should have been devoted to 'Sex and Intellect: a Feminist View'.

She frowned, trying to focus her concentration. The article had worried her, even before Wankel. She wondered why the WAG executive had asked her to write it. She was competent enough to deal with 'Intellect'; but 'Sex'. She rubbed the end of her rather pointed nose with the flat back of her hand, and adjusted her gold-rimmed glasses. It was a sign of nervousness.

Underneath the half page of 'Wankels' she wrote her own name, carefully and plainly: 'L. Suzie Highman'. It was easy, she thought, to write your own name. 'L. Suzie Highman'; she wrote it again. But what did it mean? The people who thought the problem of existence was the 'why' were wrong. The basic question was the 'who'.

She wrote it once more, L. Suzie Highman, and next to it the word 'SEX'. But she crossed that out quickly, decisively. Compared to Ego, Sex was a minor problem. Freud had thought differently; but Freud had been a man. Ego, for a woman, was all. For if I do not know who I am, how can I stand for anything? Or against anything? She went to write her name again, but paused after the 'L'. This time I shall write it out fully, because my whole name adds up to what I am; the parts I use, the parts I don't use. She wrote, lightly at first then going over it again in heavy black letters, 'LILIAN SUZIE HIGH-MAN'. What a difference the mere use or non-use of part of your name made. L. Suzie? Or Lilian S.? (Hi, Suzie! Cuppa coffee? Seat?.... Hello, Lilian. Won't you sit down? Would you like?.... Hey, Lil! C'mon, Lil! Park yer bum, Lil! Ah! Lil!....)

What can be done with a name like Lil? A blousy, back-stairs brothel kind of name, unfit to pass the holy lips of village vicars at a christening, branding the innocent forehead of the child with future guilt, slinking with the blessed water down into the hell-dark anonymity of the font.

Lil. Suggestive of teeth and tits and a wet cigarette stuck to

I decide I will wear the shirt, open to the second button, and the antique silver chain around my neck.

Thus do such affairs begin.

Suzie said, 'We'll have to get a lodger.'

A slow, rhythmical crunching sound answered her from behind the unfurled banner of the *Financial Times*. She waited. The paper shook slightly, creating a small current of air which wafted from Larry's side of the breakfast bar to hers, over the cooling toast.

'Larry.'

The edge of the paper moved down slightly, to reveal a pair of gold-rimmed glasses identical to hers. Larry said, 'OK.'

The paper moved back into place. Suzie pushed her brown hair behind her ears and leaned forward, her elbows, bare below the bell sleeves of her padded housecoat, pushing up the corner of the raffia table mat.

'You see, we have no choice.' She was being firm, reasonable, the way she had told herself she would. 'The bills; the mortgage. You know? We must find ourselves a lodger. I mean, there's no shame in having a lodger. Lots of people have lodgers nowadays. Look at Herbie Greengage; he and Miriam have a lodger, a student; so helpful; he even babysits.'

'We haven't got a baby.'

'I mean, it'll be someone in the house when I'm at WAG meetings. As long as whoever it is doesn't want the radio on. You know I can't concentrate with the radio. I need complete quiet. But we have no choice; the bills, the mortgage. Don't you think, Larry? Don't you agree?'

The newspaper came down again slowly, almost ceremonially, like the ritual furling of a sunset flag. Larry said, 'What is it with you Suzie? What is it?'

The No.14, City via Witton, was late. Suzie wriggled her shoulders as if trying to burrow further into the protection of her

15

fake fur jacket, and watched her breath under the street lights curl tentatively outwards in yellow-spittled tongues. She thought of going home. Five minutes – less if she hurried – and she could be safe again within the sanctuary delineated by her green front door.

The word 'sanctuary' came into her head quite naturally. She felt tonight like one of a species of threatened bird. She looked quite bird-like, standing under the street light in her jacket of yellow-grey fur, her shoulders hunched like bony wings and her face, rather pinched, the nose chiselled beak-sharp by shadow. And without her glasses (left off for the occasion) she had the strange, naked, vulnerable look of a young bird; even her eyes in the half light seemed round and questioning.

She thought, shall I go home, but idly, without energy, a predetermined exercise whose pattern ought to be adhered to. Shall I go home? My article, needing to be written; my books, needing to be read; a dozen things behind that green front door clamouring for attention, needing to be done. It was strange how just being brought on you such weight, such responsibilities.

She stamped her feet to bring some life into them and the pavement, dark and cold, absorbed the sound. Her feet were rather big to be supported by her narrow ankles. And uncertain in her higher-than-usual heels, she kept her knees unnaturally straight. Her legs themselves were thinnish, pale flesh cladding narrow bone. She looked, she was, a bird; awkward, ungainly, out of her usual habitat, caught in the inhospitable crosswind of the street.

When the bus came, blurred with dirt and rattling deep within itself like a bronchial pensioner, Suzie got on. As it pulled away she thought again, shall I go home, unaware that her brain was circling like a prerecorded tape, as uselessly. Shall I go home? For as the cold that silted up her veins began to melt in the thick heat of the interior, the nervousness which had been caught up by the cold and crystallized, spread out within her until each cell and every nerve trembled with it, and her 'Shall I go home?' became the raft on which she navigated past the thoughts she did not want to recognize, the half-submerged desires which she ignored, the hours of argument exchanged inside the chamber of her head, the logical and right decisions which now floated away from her, their influence washed out by the single undeniable current of self will: I will see Wankel. I will. I will.

The bus was slowing, and the man she was not aware of sitting by was waiting to get past. The man was large and black and smelled of foreign sweat and canteen food. She hurried out her legs to let him pass but not before his hand had rested briefly on her shoulder and his buttocks, shining moons of denim, had leered into her half-turned face.

She stifled the shudder which her liberal upbringing would not allow, while the man stood by her in the aisle and grinned at her out of the corner of his eye, thinking lascivious thoughts of thin white women.

If I had my glasses on I could stare him down. If my hair were closer to my ears, my mouth not drawn into this definite shape, so full. If! If! If!

She decided she would use him somehow in her article on sex and intellect. There were a lot of black feminists, she ought not to leave them out. She tried to pinch her lips into themselves, knowing they were full and wide, incongruous against her thinness. She did not like her lips. She felt they were a banner she carried to proclaim some cause in which she did not believe. Besides, their fullness was unnatural, manufactured, so her mother used to say, by sucking on her dummy until she was six. Only the thinness was her genuine self; the mouth was grafted on to her by circumstance.

She felt a sudden surge of strong dislike, but whether for herself or for she whose carelessness had caused this mouth, so out of place, so misleading, she did not know. And mingled with it was a sense of righteous injury. How pleasurable, in an odd way, to have been wronged by circumstance. How perversely good it felt to be able to lay the blame for her own imperfections at someone else's door. Perhaps she could incorporate the

notion into 'Sex and Intellect'. She made a careful mental note
to try.

The black man with the buttocks got off the bus while Suzie
was thinking. She did not notice and was vaguely surprised as
she stared into the space where he had been. She turned quickly
and peered out of the grimy window, a small dart of panic
entering her, in case she had missed her stop.

But she had not. The Town Hall's imitation Parthenon
loomed lit and garish at the far end of the street. She gave
passing thanks to the God she did not believe in but immediately became afraid of other things such as Wankel. The thought of
him being there unfurled little tongues of tension over the
surface of her skin; the thought of him not being there exploded
small grenades of shame which seemed to sever strategic nerves
and muscles until she got up and off the bus and walked over to
the curved stone steps by instinct only.

But on a different level her mind was functioning. Like a
plane caught silvery above the clouds, it moved forward
through the ordinary actions of ticket and glove and bag, of
scanning the waiting figures on the top step, of registering and
discarding them. And all the time some other element of her
mind was racing uncontrollably, a train down an unguarded
track, I wonder, I wonder, I wonder. But what she was wondering and how and where it would end, she did not know.

'Five minutes, love.'

'What?'

'They'll be starting in five minutes.'

'Oh. Yes. Thank you.'

The man at the door nodded and grinned encouragingly at
her over the high-buttoned collar of his tunic coat. He knew
them all, the types who waited at the door until the last minute,
wondering if they were going to be let down. And he always felt
sorry for those who, as the music struck up and the opening bars
drifted out from the high-ceilinged concert hall into the nearly
deserted street, slunk solitary away into the shadows. He could
always pick them, the ones who were going to be let down. This
one now (he watched covertly as Suzie shifted uneasily from one

foot to the other); this one; she would be all right. Decent enough looking young woman, nothing fancy, bit on the thin side; old – or young – enough to be his daughter; probably waiting for her husband, late out of the office. Clean cut sort of bloke most likely; suit, black vinyl brief case with a combination lock, and a worsted overcoat. Nothing – he tilted his nose sideways in disgust – nothing like this one coming up now. This was a nancy-boy if ever he saw one; he'd stake his grandma's life on it. One of those poofters. He hadn't noticed a friend waiting, but these queers were a queer lot; they even went to concerts on their own. What could you expect?

When Wankel walked up to Suzie and smiled at her the doorman teetered so far back on his heels that he was in danger of overbalancing. But as he took their tickets and stared disapprovingly over the top of Suzie's head, he thought, it didn't do to let these things rattle you. But you never could tell. And that was Gawd's truth. You never could tell.

Wankel was wondering why he was there. He suffered from claustrophobia, and concert halls, and crowds, always brought on a bad attack. He was, he thought, too sensitive all round. He had always been sensitive. He remembered how, as a small child, he had listened at a keyhole and heard his mother and his aunts talking about how sensitive he was. But even then it had given him a kind of pleasure to hear himself so described. It sounded fine, different; as if he existed on a separate plane from ordinary individuals. Of course it had had its uncomfortable side, like being bullied in the playground, taunted on the football field. But as he grew older he came to realize that not only was it pleasant, usually, to be considered sensitive, but for him it was essential. For what is a poet without his sensitivity? A mere versifier, a literary charlatan, worthy only of derision.

Tonight Wankel was feeling particularly sensitive; and more than a little disgruntled. The concert was of medieval music, and he disliked medieval music. Suzie, he had seen at first glance, was looking very ordinary, rather leggy and bedraggled, like a nestless bird. There would be no time, after the concert, to go over to the wine bar next to the Fighting Cock and make his declaration. He began to wonder, as he settled into his seat so far under the overhanging balcony that it seemed the weight of the whole building was pressing on him, whether it was all worth it. What exactly was or was not worth what, he did not define. The general thought reflected a general mood. One of his wives was seeking extra maintenance; a reading he had been engaged to give to the Perry Hall Young Communists Literary Comrades had been cancelled in favour of a darts night; and *Critical Monthly* had returned his latest poem on the grounds that it was too esoteric. Wankel parted his lips in his best imitation of a sneer. He would not let them get the better of him. He would –

He saw that Suzie was looking at him, and became aware that he was showing his crooked tooth. The sneer twisted uncomfortably into a kind of Byronic leer, which drew from Suzie no other response than a look. Wankel thought huffily, how like a woman, and stared ahead of him. The third cornet played a C sharp that wasn't. Wankel groaned. He felt Suzie's stiff shoulder make arid contact with his own. A cold bitch at heart, he thought; O God, why do you do it to me?

Suzie, sitting tight into her seat so that the harsh pile of the nylon velvet prickled the backs of her thighs, was aware, chiefly, that her poet smelled of sweat. Not a fresh, human, fleshy sweat which was – which could be – strangely more than acceptable. No, this was a stale, neglected, ground into the fabric kind of sweat, which caused her to draw into herself in distaste, harden against him. And when he took out his leather-covered notebook and began to scribble, earnestly and at a furious rate, she could watch him dispassionately. Nothing about him disturbed her now; he was rather grey and balding. It was just as well. Sex and intellect. She adjusted her glasses on her nose which was beginning to shine in the heat of the concert hall. It was probably just as well. She and Wankel would have a relationship of intellect alone. Intellectual relationships were undoubtedly of a superior kind. It would be better all round; less disturbance, less complication. Perhaps life, after all, could be less frightening than she had thought.

But on the distant battlefield beyond all rational thought struggled the still-warm corpse of her desire, unacknowledged but refusing to lie down; on its side that perverse determination which insists the object of desire is still desirable, which will not give up, which, having once decided, must possess.

Of all this Suzie was not, or would not be, aware. She sat with a bland expression on her face listening to a bland interpretation of the music while Wankel shifted and scratched and scribbled beside her.

After, when they came out stiffly into the cold, damp air, their conversation, as her poet dutifully walked her to the bus stop, was polite. Yet she felt towards him somewhat warmer. Perhaps it was the reflected glow of the interval gins. Or the prospect of the green front door behind which was contained her waiting Sex and Intellect; her waiting Lanky Larry.

When she offered her cheek for a single goodnight kiss, things went, as they often seem to do, awry, and lip met lip. They drew apart. Suzie pushed up her glasses and looked at Wankel. Wankel covered his crooked tooth and looked at Suzie. He said, 'Tomorrow?'

And she said, 'Yes; yes.'

He took her long hand in his long hand and they stood, not speaking, waiting for the bus to come.

2

If she were not my friend, it would not matter. But what is a friend for? A friend in need is a friend indeed; in adversity, you soon know who your friends are; true friendship is beyond price. And so on, and so on.

Our situation is, of course, a little different; for not only am I Lil's friend, I am her alter ego. And although I am her friend, sometimes I think I would like to be without her. For we exist in an uneasy harmony, which shifts from slumbering tolerance to a pure conflict, the flames of which may someday ignite a conflagration, and consume us both. But to sever our connection would be difficult, inhabiting as we do not only the same house, but the same flesh.

Our relationship just now is fraught, for we cannot agree about the poet. I do not want it to happen, had thought it was impossible, we two having for some time been joined, unlike before, in a commonality of character and principle.

But Lil thinks otherwise, although she has not told me. We have not talked of it at all. For of all things, a poet. Impractical, effete; and the look of him! Lil has always been attracted to men of stature, men of muscle and solidity. This one is quite short, it seems to me, though Lil who is taller than I am thinks that he is taller still. But in a way, that is worse. For what use can there be in a man who appears short, even though he is tall?

And a poet. Who will find the underwear, the car keys, purses, pens, which Lil and I continually mislay? For we are both equally forgetful. She of course is married and her husband is a gem and finds all her lost things. I am not married though I have a man who says that he is mine and asks me, am I his – knowing that I belong to no one, not even to myself. 'Lilian,' he says sometimes; and 'Lilian?' as if he did not understand. Yet he must know that I am Lilian, white flower held in a white hand, each cell untouched and pure, yes, pure though my flesh falls putrefying into the grave of my death.

*

Suzie is dreaming. You can tell she is dreaming. Her eyes, behind the pale transparency of the closed lids shift in a rhythmical yet random way. Her face in sleep has lost some of its sharpness. She resembles, as all sleepers do, a younger version of herself, one which combines youthful optimism with its prerequisite, youthful innocence. And what better place for optimism than in a dream? For in dreams, all can be accomplished.

Suzie is dreaming of her poet, or rather of his eyes. It is as if his eyes were disembodied, dark discs beyond which she can see nothing. Yet she must see beyond. Something important is there, she does not know what, but it seems to be a piece out of her own puzzle. Some element of herself which once discovered will complete her.

For in her dream she is a hollow doll. Her legs and arms move regimented in relation to each other, and her head turns from side to side. At intervals a sound squeezes past her set lips, a sound distorted, perhaps it is 'Mama'. She stares into the huge opacity of the poet's growing eyes, so large that they are now her whole horizon, she is standing on their lower lid, the rim of some half-known eternity. And like a time-traveller she steps off and falling, screams something; something. And slowing, stopping as if a giant brake had been applied, she sees no revelation, only Larry, who takes from her hand the doll she is now holding and rocks it crooning in the crook of his arm. He does not see her; he is looking at the doll and smiling, a soft, silly smile.

'Larry', she says, her voice high and piping like a demanding child's, 'Read to me; read to me.'

The voice seems to be coming from the doll. She is suddenly afraid; the feeling swells somewhere in the region of her chest and hangs there. But Larry, still smiling at the doll, says, 'Which book?'

And she, hearing her voice as if it were on the other side of a great universe, asks for the rabbit with the green umbrella carried out to sea on a rising wind.

And so he begins, his voice meshing to her conscious ear until the world exists only in his words and she drifts on them with the rabbit and the green umbrella out to meet a waiting, deeper sleep.

But at that moment strange and indefinable of change, the rabbit's face dissolves into the poet's and they are falling, he and she, the green umbrella's parachute trailing flaccid behind them, falling helpless into the vortex of the dark.

The knuckles of Wankel's mother's hands were swollen. Both her index fingers curved outwards from the thumb, denying the elegance which should belong to the fingers' extension of the palm, veering stubbornly away, making the hands look sometimes as if they could take ugly, fumbling flight. They were clasped now together in her lap, still between the intermittent bouts of rubbing.

'Why do you rub them, Mother?' said Wankel. 'You know it only makes them worse.'

Wankel's mother lifted her hands slightly before her, attempting a deprecating flutter. They wallowed for a moment like huge, ugly moths.

'Oh, you know how it is, Son. But don't you worry about me; don't you worry about your mother.'

Wankel grunted and fingered his crooked tooth, wondering how soon he could decently take his leave of her. Soon. It was gone six o'clock and a thin mist had already settled over the streets. His mother wouldn't like to see him out late in a mist. He had once had bronchitis as a child and she still insisted his chest was weak.

He gave her the daily paper which he had forgotten to do and about which she had not reminded him, not wanting to be a bother. Wankel's mother never wanted to be a bother to anyone. Her not wanting to be a bother was as insidious as water dropping on stone; it wore away all those around her, hollowed them out until they were nothing but husks blowing on the wind of her self-sacrifice.

Wankel said 'I'll get you some tea, Mother,' squeezing past the unnatural hard whiteness of her national health smile.

'Don't you bother –' she began, but Wankel shut the kitchen door against it, not quite succeeding in keeping it out, although whether he really heard the words or whether his anticipation of them rattled a well-worn groove inside his brain, is uncertain.

The kitchen brought on an attack of claustrophobia. It was so small, so narrow. Quickly, he filled the aluminium kettle and put it on the gas ring, resolving, as he did each time he boiled the kettle for his mother, to buy her an electric one, sometime.

He fussed about the kitchen getting out his mother's mug which she would use, despite the unhygienic cracking of its glaze, because it had a fading picture of the Coronation on its side. The whole kitchen had an unhygienic feeling about it which disturbed Wankel. It was not precisely dirty; but it was not precisely clean. And Wankel, though not fanatical, prided himself on being precise about the home, and about the kitchen in particular. One of his wives had once accused his carefully chosen furniture design of being clinical. And if that care for order did not extend as far as his own person, and if the sweat that Suzie had detected at the concert was, rather than an unconscious mechanism of her self-defence, a fact, then it was merely that his Art was put before his Person. For though an untidy room may be a brake to inspiration, an ill-timed bath will surely shatter the delicately balanced rhythm of a verse. And Wankel did relish, in a personal way, the idea of the careless Bohemian. A jug of wine, a knotted scarf about the neck, and thou. . . .

The kettle whistled at him drearily. This whole house was dreary: the kettle, the kitchen, his mother's mug, his mother. He hated her knotted hands, her knotted mind. And when he took the tea in to her and she sat drinking it and eating her two sweetmeal biscuits and seeking out imaginary husks of wheat with her tongue and spitting them indiscreetly into the hearth where they sizzled and writhed, then he hated that too. He tried to analyse what it was about her that made his flesh shrink away from his skin in a kind of useless, senseless cowering. He thought the problem was, he could not reconcile his mother with his Art.

25

For Art, as all true artists understood, was concerned with the heart of things, with what was important. And his mother was a living example of the trivial. But he was born of her and sometimes, when he was feeling rather down as he was tonight, he wondered whether a little of her triviality might not have been bred into him. But as soon as he was up again, he knew such thoughts were nonsense. About the stature of his mind there could be no doubt: he was Wankel.

But to his mother he was Son, which put him at a disadvantage. And she was not even a reader, she had never read a word of what he wrote. He was quite glad, because he knew she would not understand his work, any more than she understood himself. But the fact increased the space between them, until they were like two planets between which the void has severed all communication. They merely sat reflecting off each other, sending random messages, the paths of which occasionally crossed, but whose each meaning could not be deciphered by the other.

'Are you comin' home fer Christmas, Son?' she asked, the sweetmeal crumbs bobbing gently on the folded parchment of her chin.

Christmas!

'Is it December?'

Wankel made a point of never knowing, if he could avoid it, which month was which. His mother cackled loudly and suddenly, and fluttered her twisted hands. He decided he would write a poem about them, sometime. He said, 'I don't know. About Christmas; I don't know.'

His lip curled slightly, showing his crooked tooth; for what was Christmas but a bourgeois spectacle?

His mother said something which sounded like 'what about Easter?', but perhaps it was Esther, one of his wives had been Esther, his last wife.

'I don't know,' he said, the safe answer to both possibilities.

They sat staring at the fire until she began to grind her teeth and he could tolerate it and her no longer, and he said, 'Well. . . .' and told her to take care of herself, and got up, and as he was going she said, 'Don't you worry about me, Son; don't you worry about your mother.'

Herbie Greengage had been Suzie's lover. It was a long time ago, her first and only besides Larry, and no one spoke about it much. But occasionally Suzie did cast sideways thoughts towards the might-have-been. For Herbie, pimply in their mutual youth, and reaching only to Suzie's ear even in elevated shoes, was a Success. He had a large Rolls-Royce and a small and heavy-breasted wife. He had retained his hair; his belly was still flat. Only his Jewishness, which in the past he had so vehemently denied, had overtaken him.

He now made free with is oi-vehs and his mama-mias, sported a solid gold star of David on the dark chest hairs which sprouted, with only the occasional hint of grey, from between the pearlized buttons of his pure silk shirt.

Herbie Greengage's little wife called herself Miriam. Some said she had been christened Mary and a Catholic, and Herbie's mother had put on her a Jewish Mama's curse because of it. Suzie could not understand why it should matter, being herself an atheist and entirely free, in any case, of the taint of anti-Semitism. She could still recall Herbie's embarrassment when quite early in their relationship she had bought him a St Christopher for his birthday. And her astonishment when her father, asked in an undervoice what he thought of the washed and brushed and newly-presented Herbie, had hissed that he rather thought he was a Jew.

Suzie, preparing meatballs and gefüllte fish as the Greengages were expected to dinner, heaved one of her sighs. Suzie's sighs were not just sighs, they were special. A whole world of sighs of diverse shapes and nationalities compressed into one small, damp, self-pitying exhalation of air.

I could be living like that now, she thought, like her. It was unusual for Suzie to think such thoughts; she was not by nature envious. But this morning Larry had drawn further than ever

27

behind his newspaper; she had turned down two prospective lodgers; and Wankel had not telephoned her.

It would only have taken a 'yes' in place of a 'no'; and that 'yes' to the traditionally most welcome of all questions. She remembered it quite well, it was on the steps of the Geography department; they had been students together at a provincial university. 'Will you?' he had said. 'Will you?' The most welcome of questions. But even then Suzie's as yet unhardened feminism had detected in Herbie the porker-est of chauvinist pigs. What had revealed it to her? The way he had always held doors open? The way he had insisted on going with her to the launderette, and then refused to spin his shirts? Or was it the way he had approached her sexually, as if she were a half-wrapped candy bar? She shuddered and dropped a partly formed meatball on the floor. Sex. It always came down to that. Perhaps she should use her experience of Herbie in 'Sex and Intellect'. There must, after all, be some Jewish feminists.

She began to consider whether she should dress for dinner. A clean pair of jeans? For Miriam, or Mary, or whatever she called herself, always 'dressed'. Twenty-two and a pert little bum; was life never fair? And the baby had not dropped her bosom half an inch. Suzie prodded the final meatball with her kitchen fork and wondered what Wankel would make of Miriam's intellect. For Miriam's intellect, unlike her bosom, was not large. But what need did she have of intellect when she had eyelashes? Miriam had been a promotional cigarette girl until she retired at twenty, and the gale caused by her fluttering lids had fanned up many a hopeful flame. But all that was in the past. She had settled down to duty and dinners and never been detected in a single indiscretion.

Suzie had sometimes wondered about their lodger. But he was such a quiet, inoffensive little boy; no more than seventeen and very Left. Herbie laughed and said he would grow out of it. It was true, thought Suzie, that she and all her friends were much less Left than they had been at twenty (it was one of the things which added spice to Wankel, his delightful eccentricity in shouting Trotskyite slogans before the blue gates of the

Conservative Club). But she had not yet veered so far off course as to be regarded Centre. And there was something rather deep in Herbie's lodger's eyes. Miriam? Or Molotov cocktails manufactured in the disused basement of Herbie's large, secluded house? Suzie decided she would mention Herbie's lodger's name tonight, and watch Miriam closely for reaction.

What she would do if her hardly believed conjecture ever became certainty, she did not know. It was nothing to her if Miriam had a lover. Yet in a strange way she would feel her poet justified. There was no logic in it, merely the contemplation of another's crime often diverts suspicion from one's own. And although Suzie had committed nothing, yet she felt the need for her mind to be diverted from itself, from the shadow of intention there which she did not wish to contemplate; like the dark shape of a cloud, etched by the sun onto an empty field.

When Miriam's Herbie's Rolls purred up to the green front door, and the neighbours' curtains twitched and swayed on both sides of the street, Suzie did not know whether to be gratified or not. On the one hand it was nice to cause a stir; but on the other, and under Wankel's recent influence, Suzie felt the car was too impossibly bourgeois, and Herbie should distribute it, and his other profits, to the poor.

She decided she would tell him so at an appropriate point during dinner. But it was not so simple. For, as Suzie saw when she moved forward to the door with only a marginally insincere smile of welcome on her lips, they had brought the baby.

'So awful,' said Miriam in her youthful breathy way, 'these sitters! And the lodger, out at a Marxist rally. So – so inconsiderate!'

Her voice had a high-pitched little-girlness to it, as if her lungs were situated somewhere towards the bridge of her nose.

'But you won't mind now, Suzie, will you?' said Herbie, stroking Miriam's fox fur affectionately, and looking down at the baby in a silly, doting way.

Suzie mouthed appropriate platitudes as she ushered them into the small, red hallway. She hated all children. She hated how they dribbled and puked and were everywhere with their sticky, pokey fingers. But a guest is a guest. And if her 'not-at-alls' and 'hasn't-he-growns' would have sounded hollow to an attentive ear, Miriam and Herbie, overflowing with the pride of creation of this unique and portable possession, did not notice.

Herbie said, 'You've done your hall. Red, too. Isn't it a little Freudian?' Suzie stared at him. He grinned, showing his gold fillings, and patted her on the shoulder. 'You know. Like a vagina; red; warm.'

Miriam tittered and said 'Oh, Herbie!' managing at the same time both to censure and to smirk. Herbie smiled a fond, coy, satisfied, possessive smile. Then, remembering too late his old affair with Suzie, snatched his hand away from her shoulder as if her flesh had suddenly caught fire, and poked a playful finger into the baby's belly, who immediately began to cry.

'Where's Larry?' asked Herbie as they went in, raising his voice over the baby's gathering roar. 'In the kitchen, hey? Cooking? You found yourself a treasure there, you sure did!'

He said it in a half-joking, half-patronizing way, and Suzie thought, as she always thought when she was with Herbie, how his assumed Americanisms grated on her. Herbie was going to go to the States. The States were where the action was, the only place to succeed. But Suzie had long ago decided it was talk, just talk. She pushed her glasses more firmly on to her nose and said, 'When are you going to the States, Herbie?'

He said, 'I think I'll go see Larry in the kitchen.'

He opened the kitchen door and Larry said 'balls', and as he shut it behind him Suzie said, 'Meatballs; he's warming them up.'

Miriam said, 'Will you just hold Benjie a minute while I powder my nose?' and smiled winningly at Suzie as she handed over the writhing, screaming crochet bundle.

Twenty-two and a pert bum! Was life never fair?

The candles were burning low into their holders. The smoke from Herbie's Monte Cristo Habana hung in little feathery halos just outside the twin spheres of light which jumped and fluttered round their lengthening flames. Suzie liked to dine by candle light; she had read somewhere that it was chic. But she felt tonight as if the candle light produced a weird effect, as if the tapering flames had turned them all to puppets, jerking on unseen strings. Or perhaps it was more truly like a silent picture, where everyone moves in a queer stiff way, each turn of head or wrist separate from the one before, each look and every gesture isolated, exaggerated.

Herbie, chewing inelegantly on his cigar, broke a silence. 'The gefüllte fish was fine, Larry, just fine.'

Suzie said, 'I prepared it.'

'Oh, sure, sure.' Herbie belched gently and wiped his mouth on Miriam's table napkin. He was beginning to be a little drunk. 'And the meatballs; fine; fine. You're a good cook, Larry.'

Suzie said, 'I prepared them.'

'Oh? Sure, sure. D'you mind if I help myself to a little more wine?' He reached for the bottle and poured from it untidily, so that some drops spilled onto the polished surface of Suzie's reproduction dining table. It was fashionable, Suzie believed, to dine without a cloth. Herbie mopped up the moisture vaguely with the abused napkin and settled himself more comfortably behind his glass.

'Y'know, it really is great t'see you two together; your co-operation; division of labour. Now me and Miriam, we operate the same; don't we, Miri? Don't we, Sweeting?'

Miriam looked puzzled but pouted prettily, showing just the very edges of her small white teeth. 'Do we, Herbie?'

'Why, sure we do!' chuckled Herbie, enjoying his joke. 'I labour, and you divide the profits. A-haw, a-haw.'

Larry said, combing his fingers through his beard, 'Suzie's an ardent feminist.'

'Larry my boy –' Herbie was expansive, confidential, patronizing, all at the same time, 'She always was; she al-ways was. A-haw, a-haw.'

'But how can Suzie be a feminist when she doesn't wear make-up?'

'No, Littlest!' Herbie reached round the table leg and patted

31

indulgently the full curve of her thigh. 'Feminist, not Feminine. The one's the opposite of the other. A-haw, a-haw.'

Suzie, through the fumes of wine which were beginning to rise like marsh-mists in her brain, wondered why she was being talked about, rather than to. It disturbed her. I suppose I do exist, she thought. I suppose I am really here. She clasped her hands together one against the other to prove she still felt and could feel. But her doubts only increased, for the skin of her arm seemed to her own touch papery and lifeless; and her hands, as she watched them move, seemed distant from her, as unconnected to herself as if she were a disinterested observer.

She sat for what could have been quite a long time, trying to apportion fairly how much of their fault in talking of rather than to her was really her own, a result of doubting her actual existence there at the table. Then she said to no one in particular and with careful emphasis, 'I am a person.'

There was a short silence. Miriam giggled and Herbie grinned and nodded like a clockwork dog.

'Sure, y'are Suzie. We all are. Persons. Here's to us all, persons every one. (Can I help myself to a little more wine? Thank you; thank you.)'

Miriam opened her eyes very wide and seemed about to say something but Herbie interrupted her.

'Why don't you have some cheese, Sweetie? This cheese is real good, what is it Suzie? Gorgonzola? Ah, Stilton! Good old English Stilton. One thing the English can still do, make good cheese.'

Suzie was about to say, 'You're English too', but he had begun to sing 'There'll Always Be An England' in an off-key falsetto which woke the baby, who began to cry.

Miriam got up to see to Benjie. Larry got up to fetch another bottle. The telephone rang loudly and unexpectedly, like the bell marking the end of an inconclusive boxing match. Suzie got up to answer it on legs which felt longer than usual, stork-like. It seemed a long way to the hall, dim under its fringed red shade. And the hall, the telephone, herself, all seemed odd, unreal, like a poorly executed lantern slide.

It was Wankel, very esoteric, reading his latest poem in breathy, irregular phrases to a background of recorded flute.

Suzie leaned against the Freudian red of the hall wall and began to giggle, a small bubbling of sound deep within her, which swelled over her lips in one great uncontrollable surge of laughter. And the tears which spilled over her eyelids and ran down her face and into her mouth tasted salty and warm.

'I must be here,' she said out loud. 'I can taste my tears.'

Somehow the thought made her laugh even more. Wankel turned off the flute music and said, injured and uncomprehending, 'What's the matter with you, Suzie? What's wrong?'

Much later, when Miriam and Herbie and the portable Benjie had gone, and the house had settled into a preternatural quietude, and the smells of meatballs and gefüllte fish had begun to settle and stale, Suzie lay on her back in the bed which occupied nearly the whole of their small bedroom, and contemplated the lie. It was not a large lie. But it was a lie which hung somewhere above her supine form, a tangible area of dark within the dark, a peculiar kind of pressure in the air whose essence seemed to be distilled into a pure guilt which set and crystallized like a malignancy inside her brain. But I have done nothing, she thought, nothing. Only to say Wankel was not Wankel. There was something almost biblical in her denial of him.

But no cock had yet crowed. There was only the imperfect silence of the city night, and Larry's irregular breathing on the pillow next to hers. And the echo, in her head, of her own voice, round which her wine-slacked lips had formed not 'Wankel' but 'wrong number; wrong number; wrong number'.

It was a long time before she slept, a fitful and uneasy sleep in which she dreamed that on the roof above the green front door settled a giant cockerel of beady and defiant eye, whose call, audible even as far away as Lazarus Street and beyond, sounded high and clear the triumphant announcement, 'Wankel-doo-del-doooooo'.

*

33

Wankel's rooms were in the crumbling basement of a crumbling house in the Edwardian area of the city where the students lived. It was inconvenient to get to. You had to catch two buses and walk quarter of a mile to go anywhere at all.

But Wankel liked it. It suited his notion of the Bohemian, and besides, it was a constant reminder of the decadence and downfall of the bourgeoisie.

If you did not know Wankel, if he were just anyone, you might wonder whether you could detect in his manner as he showed you the oak, the sash, the intricate tiling of the fireplace, the elaborate carving of the cornices which luxuriate and define the high, broad ceilings – you might wonder whether you could detect a touch, not of the contempt which would be fitted to his egalitarian principles, but of that other, gentler emotion, the lust for possession of the admired.

For Wankel did admire his rooms. He admired their fine proportions, which allowed him to move and breathe in comfort. He admired the solidity of the walls, how they mellowed and absorbed all sharp, intrusive sound, until he could imagine, as he sat in the evenings with his slippered feet resting on the single luxury of his velvet-covered footstool, and listened to his favourite Bach cantata, that he lived in a more gracious age, where tall men did not jostle short men in a cafeteria queue; where women were conveniently subdivided into mistresses and wives; and where poets had patrons and occupied their rightful position of importance in the scheme of things.

But he secretly despised this weakness in himself; he would have liked to scorn in their entirety these trappings of bourgeois supremacy; but he could not. It was, he supposed, not without a feeling of complacency, the artist in him. And after all, when the glorious revolution came, artists would surely be a special case.

And in the meantime he salved his left-wing conscience by furnishing his rooms even more sparsely than his dole money decreed; and by denying vehemently, even to himself, the wish that these rooms did belong to him, and he to them; the knowledge that if he owned them he would never give them to the poor, that he would have and savour and become them every bit as much as any Edwardian gentleman whose gains, ill-gotten out of proletarian sweat, were spent on the pleasures of practical self-enrichment.

But if Wankel was coy concerning his materialist desires that coyness did not extend as far as the simpler, more readily admissible lusts of the flesh. He was sitting now, lusting away a morning which should rightfully have been devoted to his Art, thinking in particular of Suzie, in general of how abundant was the flesh for which he lusted, how accessible, in streets, in bars, in the darkened balconies of concert halls, in theatre foyers, at post-rehearsal parties, at readings, at writers' groups, on the other end of telephones, in newspapers, in magazines, on television, on tape; but most of all in the infinitely variable collection of images which he carried within his brain, the inexhaustible parade of shape and size and touch and taste which he could combine at will in endless and fascinating variation.

'My imagination', breathed Wankel reverently. 'My imagination'.

There were times, he was willing to admit, when imagination was more satisfying than reality. Flesh in the flesh had a habit of being wayward. The flesh you wanted was unavailable. The flesh you didn't want cried on your doorstep at 10 p.m. And the flesh that you wanted and was available often became, on closer inspection, unwantable. An ill-placed mole, hanging like a dried, discoloured leech upon the neck; a bony shoulder blade; an over-solid thigh; sometimes even as little as a misshaped ear lobe, set too low behind the jaw, creating an impression of bovine stupidity. Such simple things could douse desire as efficiently as water cast on flame.

But his imagination air-brushed out such imperfections, rendering the flesh as faultless as a Botticelli Venus. And the flesh contained within his mind was so obliging, so malleable to his every wish; no moods, no tantrums; no inconvenient declarations of self-will. No, that flesh was entirely in tune with his desires, wanted what he wanted, went where he went.

But sometimes, like the smallest tremor presaging an earthquake, there appeared at the edge of his mind a quiver of doubt; for was not the flesh that he imagined, being a product of his brain, merely an extension of his own? Was he, in desiring it and in consummating that desire, entering upon the vilest of vile incest – the fruit of which might one day show itself as some unspeakable aberration?

At such times he turned away from mental flesh and concentrated on the pursuit of the real. In such a mood he had discovered Suzie.

Suzie. 'Ah, Suzie!' he murmured, pausing in his dual contemplation of Bach and spaghetti bolognese to visualize her as yet untested charms.

He blinked against the steam which rose up from the bubbling pan in succulent and savoury clouds and mentally complimented himself on the production of another tasty dish. For Suzie was coming at lunchtime; and Wankel prided himself on being a cook.

There was, he thought, something infinitely sensual about food. The anticipation; the preparation; the consumption – which he preferred to be slow and deliberate, almost ceremonial – then the glorious feeling of satiation which spread from the weighted stomach out through limbs and torso until it lay on the mind, a quilting of finest down.

He took a spoonful of the thick, rich sauce, tasted it and smacked his lips. Just right! Everything this morning seemed more right than usual; he supposed he must be happy, or as happy as a poet can ever be. He had sat up until the small hours wrestling with a small poem about Che Guevara; he had lost; but the effort made him feel virtuous.

He put the lid back on the pan, adjusted the gas flame so that the sauce was barely simmering, and went into his bedroom to change. He did not usually change for women; he did not believe in it. And he felt besides that his mind held more immediate appeal for them than his body; for he had gone, marginally, to seed. It was nothing serious. A little surplus flesh in the region of buttock and hip; a slight lengthening of the muscle that had formerly connected belly to backbone; and his thighs, he wistfully acknowledged, had seen better days. But it was nothing serious. Some exercise, when he had time, would soon put him to rights.

But it was better, perhaps, not to draw attention to the area below his neck; to which end he usually entertained his women – real and imagined – in an ancient jumper and corduroy slacks. But he felt that Suzie, with her liking for medieval music and her neat little ankles, would not be impressed. And he did want to impress her. The predominance of the imaginary over the real was beginning to concern him; his seduction of Suzie's real flesh was essential to his peace of mind.

So he put on now his green shirt and turquoise tie, and arranged carefully yet casually in his breast pocket a handkerchief of spotted silk. It had been a present from some other real flesh; sent to him on his birthday, its colour an exact match to the red of a single, accompanying rose. Such whimsicality had pleased him at the time; but flesh is flesh; and he had remembered the shape and colour of the rose long after he had forgotten the shape and colour of the giver.

He hoped Suzie would be impressed. Uncertainty was unusual in him, but he was uncertain of Suzie. For she was – in some way he could not quite define – odd. He was aware that some people thought of him as odd; but poets had a right to oddity; others – and particularly women – did not.

And it was strange and disconcerting that whenever he thought about her, it was never as her ordinary self. Always he saw her as some other, foreign creature; a horse, with long, fine fragile legs and nostrils that curved and flared as it galloped away from him. Or a bird with a quick, questioning tilt to its head, and bright, round eyes which enquired of him – what, he could not say. And sometimes she was to him a cat, sleek and self-contained, casting at the world with a careless paw, dismissing it – and him – with an idle flick of tail.

So real were these images of her that it came almost as a shock when he opened the door and found her ordinary self standing on the mat, her hair blown untidily across her cheek and the end of her nose reddened with cold.

37

He saw that she had no gloves, and grasping the excuse and her hands, drew her inside saying, 'Come in, come in. Come by the fire; you must be cold.'

She answered him with a tight, brief smile which hardly moved her lips, and went in hesitantly, looking around her as if she half expected to discover some trap. It was the first time she had been to his rooms. She said, not looking at him, 'They're big.'

'What? Oh, yes; the rooms; big; quite big.'

Wankel let go of her hands because he could think of no reason for continuing to hold them. The touch of her cold, pale flesh had acted on him like adrenalin. He could feel his heart beginning to increase its pumping. And the muscles inside his legs and arms twitched and shivered. He said, 'You're cold; I'll turn up the heat,' and went and switched on the second bar of the electric fire. When he offered to take her coat she said she would keep it on. It was not really a coat; it was a curiously fluffy little jacket, knitted and much too young for her.

She stood by the window in it, silent, as if waiting for something to happen. Wankel was disconcerted. Most women wanted to rush in with small talk and compliments; and from there it was only a short step to their blushingly requesting him to sign this book, that magazine.

Suzie's silence was like the plucking of an untuned string; he wanted to end it, but she stood by the window so moulded and untouchable that he was at a loss. He said, in his confusion, the words heaping out wayward over his tongue, 'Shall I sign something?'

She swivelled her head slowly on her white neck so that she was looking at him. 'What?'

He did not know himself what he had meant, except that it was all part of the unusual confusion he was feeling because of her. But trying to establish in his brain some kind of order, he went to the bookshelf and took down a thin buff-coloured book, and hastily wrote inside the cover, and gave it to her.

She said, 'For me?'

'Yes.'

'Thank you.'

She pushed her glasses higher up on her nose; it was a sign of nervousness. Wankel said, 'Aren't you going to look inside? I've written in it.'

But she ignored the book, held it by the tips of her fingers only, murmured something, of which he caught the word 'later', and put the book away from her.

Wankel began to be irritated. He liked his gifts to be appreciated, and her offhand treatment of a book of his – his own book, his own work – nettled him. But in a way he was glad of it, for as the irritation grew, the confusion receded. He looked at her, critically, noting the incongruity of the fluffy jacket. Wankel believed he had an eye for clothes; he noticed now, for the first time, how badly Suzie dressed.

He turned his shoulder to her and, walking to the other side of the room, offered her a drink in a bored, condescending way.

'Gin?'

She nodded, and sat down on the very edge of an armless chair too far from the fire to be affected by its heat. To Wankel, watching her over the top of the tonic bottle, she seemed to be perching rather than sitting, as if she might take sudden, nervous flight. It annoyed him. He made a contemptuous snorting sound in his nose, and drank half his large brandy in one swallow. So much for real flesh. Wayward; wayward.

Yet why had she come? Was there some strange working of her mind of which he was not aware, which had caused her to come when she had rather stay away? Real flesh was strange, incomprehensible; there was no logic in it; it existed only to conceal an inner, dark, unravellable mystery.

And Wankel was not in the mood for mysteries. Mysteries would have occupied too much of the time rightfully devoted to his art; all he wanted was uncomplicated flesh. As he watched her sitting straight-backed on the straight chair examining with apparent absorption the circle described by the turning of the ankle on the foot, round, round, round, he began to doubt Suzie was that flesh. When he said, 'Lunch?' and she looked startled, as if she had forgotten he was there or she was there, or both, and refused, saying that she never ate during the day, he became convinced of it. He began to measure how much time remained to be spent with her, and to will it away. He decided he would eat without her, and went and served the carefully prepared food carelessly, and fed himself forkfuls of it in a slovenly, random way, not saying anything, pretending to be engrossed by it.

Suzie sipped dry-lipped at her drink and watched him, she hoped without seeming to, while he sucked up noisily the soft ends of the spaghetti strings, and licked the rich sauce off his chin and cheek. Little spots of it had sprayed over the turquoise material of his shirt; they looked like rusty specks of blood, like the ageing memory of her own pubescent blood. Suzie was afraid of blood; it was so – elemental.

She wondered why she was there. She thought Wankel distant, offhand. Yet why had he invited her, if he had rather she stayed away? Was there some strange working of his mind of which she was unaware? There seemed no logic in it; men were strange, incomprehensible.

She finished her drink, accepted another and swallowed it down quickly, keeping it from touching the sides of her throat like a medicine she thought was necessary but would have preferred to do without. She would have liked to move nearer the fire, but the silence which existed now between her and Wankel held her to the cold, straight chair as effectively as if she were constrained by metal ropes.

She watched Wankel push his empty plate away from him and lean his elbows on the table and stare moodily out of the long window into the unkempt garden beyond. A dog wandered up and nosed at a tussock of dry grass. Wankel hissed at it and flapped his hands. Suzie noticed how white his hands were and narrow, like a woman's; the gesture itself had been woman-like and impotent.

'Don't you like dogs?' she said.

'No; nasty, smelly, snuffly creatures.'

His face was tinged with red around the cheeks and forehead, whether caused by spiced spaghetti or annoyance, Suzie could not tell.

He had got up and gone to the window, where he rattled his knuckles on the pane and hissed again. A lock of his hair had fallen forward and hung like a tired question mark against his forehead. Suzie thought he looked rather ridiculous, like a great, cross child; yet at the same time curiously appealing, now that he was no longer contained away from her.

And that ineffectual flapping of his hand, so like a woman's, released the tightness that had settled in her, let it out as sharply and suddenly as if some metal casing had been struck and split and fallen away.

And the alcohol was beginning to blow about her brain in pleasurable little gusts. She felt much stronger, surer; more in control of herself, and so perhaps of him. She stood up.

Wankel said hopefully, 'Don't say you have to go already?'

But she shook her head and went towards him. She had unbuttoned the knitted jacket and Wankel could see the cling of her fine sweater to her body. But he was not moved by it; she was flesh, and wayward.

She stood beside him for a moment, watching the dog mooch and scratch, then fumblingly, shyly, took from her handbag a book. Wankel saw that it was one of his, his last-but-one collection, of which he was particularly proud: *Poems of Revolution and Revolt*.

Suzie pushed her glasses up on her nose and said, 'Would you sign this for me?'

Wankel took the book from her and smiled, a slow, confident, condescending smile. Then he took out his gold topped pen from his inside pocket and wrote 'For Suzie, with love from Wankel', with just the right amount of flourish. It was not the wine bar next to the Fighting Cock; but it would have to do.

This time she opened the book to see what he had written, but he did not notice, he was looking at the way her fine sweater clung to her body, and how the soft, fluffy knit of her jacket stroked at the taut skin just below her ear. As he leaned towards her, the perfume of her skin rose up to him, tantalizing, hot.

The dog paused in his nosing of the grass outside the window, and cocked his head enquiringly. But he was only a mongrel and did not understand the delicacies of the conduct of real flesh. He considered for a moment how strange was the illusion of one where previously two had been, but soon lost interest, and lifting a dismissive leg, directed a jet of pale urine unerringly against the pane.

Inside, Suzie, curbing in small, mewing protests Wankel's more ardent caresses, heard over the sucking sound of kisses the splash, and hoped it had not begun to rain.

Wankel, feeling how crushable were the bones contained within the circle of his arms, how smooth and bare the flesh beneath the clothes, felt oddly disappointed. As though this were not real flesh that he held, but the illusion of it; and what the circle of his arms contained was no more than a vulnerable, featherless bird.

3

There is such finality about the word 'husband'. Hus-bund; those alliterated 'u's' falling heavy onto the ear and mind like the thud of footsteps in a silent street, or an old door closing.

Then again, hus-bund; house-bound; has-been; a slight twist of the lips, an alteration of the tongue's position to the teeth, a relaxation or constriction of a muscle in the jaw – and there you have it.

And there I have it. For I am waiting as a good wife should, for he whom I did not at the altar (being fashionably liberated) vow to obey. Yes, waiting as a good wife should, in a tidy house with tidy hair and a tidy face. I have – as advised to by the columns of my glossy women's magazine – put on clean under-wear, in case. Quite like waiting to be called to hospital, except I do not pack anything. Rather I have just unpacked – in what for me was an unusual haste – my handbag, taken from it the book my poet has given me, containing not only his illustrious name, but the statement, perhaps less illustrious, of his love. Or so the legend would have me believe.

It is, of course, strategy. Or perhaps tactics. My chauvinistic education has ensured I cannot define the difference. And today's meeting with my poet – our third – has been conducted in the manner of a skirmish. We circle each other like hackled dogs, lamentably unsure of both our own and each other's intentions. May; may not.

As if on cue, May-who-lives-with-us bounds in and talks to me of something which I do not want to know. Ubiquitous; the May, and the may.

I will her off from me, wanting to empty and compose my mind for he who will never be obeyed; though I have nothing to reveal to him, nothing to hide; for there is no indictable misdemeanour in intention.

He comes in on a swirl of dying afternoon and kisses my forehead in a perfunctory, well-used way, and thrusting a bouquet into my unready hands disappears into the kitchen on the ebb tide of some muttered word.

I push my nose into the smell of out-of-season roses, of carnations, of the other flowers whose names I wish and mean to learn but never do. I think that I will certainly give him up, my poet, abandon him, devote myself to wifely occupations, work, and lovely Lanky Larry.

But which, I wonder, which will live the longest – resolution, or the flowers? I think by a short head it may be the flowers, which will not die for a week, possibly two.

Ah, Lil! Do not allow yourself to be deceived by love. An inky etching, achieved by the merest passing pressure of wrist and palm; such is the love your poet has inscribed for you. The crudest trap, whose trigger may be as little as the turning of a head.

Far preferable to identify and settle for lust.

And what is this difficulty people have with lust? Why the preoccupation with, insistence on, love, love, love? Or even worse, romance? I wonder at the women who are loath to admit that lust exists. For only think of all the men who in the twilight, in the back seats of cars, on illicit half-made beds, on floors, in parks, in disused bicycle sheds, say, in passion or the anticipation of it, the 'I love you' when the truth of it is the 'I lust'. A confusion of declensions learnt in the womb.

Yet how the women slobber it up like mother's milk, assuming temporary sated sleekness from its supposed veracity. 'He loves me', they say, both openly and silently within the emptiness inside their heads. And the echo of it fills them, puffs them out as if it were the source, the definition of their whole identity.

With us – my man and me – there is neither love nor lust. We exist in the vacuum between what has been, what will be.

Sometimes we touch, tangential as water over round stone; sometimes we speak, but our words are no more than the leaves' wind-lifted skeletons.

Suzie's mouth had begun to grow. She was not sure when it had begun to grow, but this morning, staring myopically into the bathroom mirror as she cleaned her teeth, she had seen it. An insidious flowering of pink on white; an overtaking by texture-lip of texture-cheek. It was as yet so slight that she was not seriously alarmed; but she had, to combat further spread, begun to control the errant area by tightening in its muscle, like the draw-string of a bag from which no cat could ever be suspected of being let out.

She had already perfected the working of it so that it hardly interfered with her speech. Although Miriam, who had called round with the baby, seemed to be having difficulty understanding her. Leaning forward conspiratorially, she said, 'Is it dentures? I know a very good man.'

Suzie shook her head; it was easier than speaking; her jaw had begun to tire.

'Larry? He hasn't been . . .?'

Miriam paused delicately; she could see no visible bruises or scars, and Larry had always seemed to her such a quiet person. But then, the quiet ones were often the worst; you never could tell. But Suzie was shaking her head again, decisively. What, then? Had she had a stroke? No, no other part of her body seemed to be affected. No drooping of the eyelid; no slowness of arm or leg. But there was definitely something wrong with her. Was she having a Breakdown?

Miriam always thought of Breakdowns with a capital 'B'. Herbie had told her that Breakdown was just a polite way of saying someone was nuts; she wouldn't be at all surpised if Suzie was nuts. All these (what had Herbie called them . . .? Ah, yes) all these feminists were a little nuts. Miriam had once read a feminist magazine while sitting in the waiting room of the Family Planning Clinic. It had been all about women in some awful country like Arabia, having bits of their genitals cut off.

She thought it was disgusting, people writing about things like that. They ought not to be allowed to. She had spoken to Herbie about it, but he had said it probably wasn't true, nothing in these feminist magazines was true; and in any case, she was not to worry; he would still love his little Miri even minus a bit of genital here or there.

She sat, while Suzie made some coffee, thinking how lucky she was to have found her Herbie. Their marriage was surely made in Heaven (she would have liked to say that to Herbie; it sounded so – sort of – poetic; but she was wary of treading on unsafe religious ground; did Jews believe in Heaven?). And Herbie was so generous; the fox fur when little Benjie came; she had better get pregnant again quickly; next time it might be a mink!

But Suzie. What she needed was someone like Herbie. That would straighten her out; no more nonsense with these Women's Groups. In Miriam's opinion, for Herbie had told her so, these Groups were nothing but trouble. Full of Thespians, too; homosexuals were bad enough, but when it came to Thespians! It was unnatural; it ought to be stopped. She wondered sometimes whether Rex, her student lodger, might not be – as she had so delicately put it to Herbie – That Way Inclined. But Herbie had pooh-poohed the idea. She frowned, a small crease marring her unmarked forehead. That was Herbie's one fault, his tendency to pooh-pooh; as if what she, Miriam, thought and said was of no account. But then, what did it matter? He was such a sweetie. And she usually got what she wanted in the end. She said, 'I haven't told you about Rex?'

'Ex?' Suzie's lips were in spasm.

'Yes, Rex; our lodger.'

''Ngo.'

Miriam plumped up her breasts between her arms as though they were twin feather cushions, and lowered her voice confidentially. 'Well, Herbie thought the generosity had gone on long enough.'

'Enerosity?'

'Yes, generosity; the lodger; sharing our home; paying

peanuts. And he said to me, wouldn't it be nice if there could be just the two of us, just for a change. So Rex is moving on.'

She patted her own plump knee in self-congratulatory triumph, and leaned back, smiling the beatific smile of a medieval virgin. 'Just us! Won't it be lovely? Herbie and me; and Baby makes three.'

Suzie said, 'I've found a lodger.'

On the other side of the gas fire, Larry's slippered feet twitched as though a nerve had been accidentally prodded. The newspaper which hid the whole of him from the waist up, shook slightly in sympathy.

'A student. His name is Ex.'

Suzie had mastered the muscle control of her mouth so well that her speech was nearly natural; but she was still having difficulty with the 'R's'. Larry said, without moving the paper, 'Ex?'

'No, Ex. Herbie's lodger.'

There was a silence. Suzie said, 'I thought it was for the best. I mean, we have to have a lodger; the bills; the mortgage; we have no choice.'

Larry turned over a page, carefully adjusting the whole back into its correct position. Suzie said, 'Larry; did you hear me?'

Larry turned over another page, the crackle of it exploding like a gunshot past the hissing of the fire.

'Larry! Why don't you answer me! Aren't you interested? Don't you care?'

Slowly, slowly, like the rising of a reluctant sun, the curve of Larry's balding head appeared from behind the newspaper. Then the forehead, smooth and apparently untroubled; then the eyebrows; then the eyes, which looked at her from behind their shutters of glass as dispassionately as if she were a specimen inside a tank. He said, thoughtfully, un-comprehendingly, 'What is it with you Suzie? What is it?'

*

47

An Englishman's home, so it is said, is his castle. But Suzie's home and Larry's, delineated by the green front door, topped by the self-effacing rise of roof (the prospect of whose re-slating causes Larry's nervous tic) – their home does not seem to them a castle.

Not that they have a sound basis for comparison. But they did once visit a genuine castle while on holiday in Scotland (blissful in the innocence of their pre-married state) and aah'd over it, and both agreed (a circumstance extinct since returning from the altar) how wonderful it would be to have a castle of Our Own.

Five years of marriage have milked dry their collective mind of dreams. Yet each harbours in the separate and as yet not wholly tainted self, a remnant of the idea. A shadow of the grand plan, it is true, but none the less a sliver of that romantic yearning for better things.

But how are their castles – so separate now that neither one knows of the other – to be achieved?

Larry's, by his keeping up with things. Which things he is keeping up with is not quite certain. But he knows that by keeping up with things, he can succeed. That is why he spends so much of his time reading newspapers; there is a great deal, in newspapers, to be kept up with.

What he is going to succeed at is unclear. As the years pass and his castle is no nearer becoming a reality, sometimes there edges into the inner sanctum of his mind, the Devil doubt. But he will not succumb to it. He hoists up the protective Cross of newsprint and devotes himself more assiduously than ever to those things with which he is keeping up.

If Larry were a banker or a barrister, Suzie's problem might not be so immediate. For position, with a man, defines identity. And women are allowed, encouraged rather, to define themselves through the position of he who delivers the financial goods.

But Larry – poor Larry, as he will be in five or six or seven years' time; the symptoms of it can already be detected in the defeated down-tilt of his shoulder bones – Larry is neither banker nor barrister, is indeed nothing but Larry. He has a job, but one to which no kudos can possibly be attached; he is probably a teacher or a representative. And the goods which he delivers are quite as meagre as his wife's.

So Suzie must define her identity and achieve her castle by herself. Her means are as various as she. She embarks on different projects, all directed to the common end. Just now her project is Putting Something By. Each week, each day, she drops through the slit back of the pig-with-eyes-like-Wankel's a silver coin. She mutters something over it (in a previous age she would certainly have been burnt as a witch) and for that moment grows sleek on the anticipation of the castle that the coin will surely buy.

The remoteness of the thing itself does not as yet concern her; for she is young, younger than Larry, much younger. And constant comparison between them allows her to believe that nothing has changed; that there is still time.

Her lodger is an extension of the putting-by. He – or rather his meagre rent – is an agent, a fulcrum which will move her world. When Suzie looks at him she sees the battlements from which she will before too long look out with such possessive pride towards the distant boundaries of her domain.

Meanwhile, her lodger is an inconvenience; the green front door less drawbridge-like than ever; the walls, so solid and Victorian, too solid, cell-like, crowding in. Suzie measures herself against a yardstick to see if she has grown; and finding no change, decides it is all in the mind. And if it is in the mind it must be, *must* be, controllable.

It was three weeks before Christmas. Suzie was standing on her head watching a piece of silver tinsel which twisted and swayed, spilling out small daggers of silver light across the ceiling above her upturned feet.

She was practising positive thinking. It was part of her strategy to overcome the bad thoughts she had had since the arrival of the lodger, the bad feelings she had been experiencing.

49

For the lodger disturbed her. Not only his presence, but the particular elements of himself which made him a uniquely recognizable individual. The way his eyes swooped, almond-shaped, towards the narrow bridge of his nose; how pale his skin was, as if it were hardly ever exposed to sunlight. Then there was the general oddness of him, how on the coldest day he would wear a summer shirt, curiously old fashioned, with wide-cut sleeves reaching nearly to his elbows; and the elbows themselves, the skin of them worn hard, patchworked into little leathery squares, quite unlike the other soft flesh of his arm, which seemed at once to have so little substance to it that it could withstand no pressure, not even so much as the grasping between finger and thumb; but at the same time to be curiously resilient, as if some elasticity had permeated into it and it, and he, were indestructible.

But Suzie was determined to overcome her disturbance. The book on positive thinking had impressed her. People had won fortunes just by thinking about it in the right way. And the lodger was a man like any other. Hadn't he lived with Herbie and Miriam? Had he disturbed *them*? No. So the problem lay with her: an evil presence in her mind which she was resolved to exorcize.

And since she had read somewhere that an increased blood flow to the brain helped thinking processes, she practised her positive thinking on her head.

It seemed as though it might be doing good. Last night when Rex had spoken to her in the kitchen, she had managed to reply without the usual quiver of distaste fingering her spine, making her want to turn away. And this morning, when she had walked past his room, where she knew from the unbroken quiet he would still be enjoying the gentle warmth of her second best duvet, she had not made the habitual detour which took her sidling up against the banisters, as far away from his door and his person as possible.

Yet despite these improvements, the thought of him weighed heavy in the house and in her mind, so that whenever she went into a room and found he was not there, a feeling of relief would

lift her spirits only to be followed by an apprehensive cal-
culation of how long she could count on his being gone.

Today she was trying to think herself out of this into an ideal
frame of mind where she would welcome his company, look for
him when he was not there.

She had been on her head for an hour and a half and had
succeeded in altering nothing. Larry had come in, changed, and
gone out, all without glancing in her direction. She had heard
Rex come in through the green front door (quietly, so quietly his
very restraint acted on her like an irritant) up the stairs and into
his room. And now the house was silent except for the whirr of
the water through the central heating pipes, and the rhythm of
her own pulse pumping loudly in her ears.

Dutifully she watched the twirl and sway of the tinsel;
dutifully she breathed in and out in regular, controlled breaths;
she schooled herself to think of every good thing possible about
her lodger; but her mind was wayward. All she could think of
was the way his hair grew low on his forehead giving him a
perpetual frown; and the way he stood in front of the cooker with
his torso relaxed into his hips so that his whole body was curved
into a single untidy slouch.

So she began to think instead of Wankel. The thought of him –
or rather the lack of him – increased her feeling of depression.
For he had been ailing with influenza and she had not seen him
for several days. She would have liked to want to take him
toddies and smooth his brow, but illness disturbed her. Sick
people seemed to assume an identity not normally their own.
She did not quite know how it was, but their exteriors became no
more than a shell, a kind of camouflage behind which spirit
battled with body, and body battled with itself.

But she had felt Wankel's lack. No telephone calls. No
accidental meetings on the library steps (he had accidentally let
her know of his regular visits to the reference room; he was
working on an anthology of Bolshevik love poetry, and was
finding sources difficult). No finger to touch finger. For since the
occasion of his rooms they had both withdrawn, like armies
reassembling for the next offensive. Life was, she felt, bleak.

And although she tried her hardest to believe in it, the tinsel on the ceiling was a bauble, powerless to help.

She sighed, and swung her legs away from the wall and lay prone on the floor feeling the blood even itself out through her body, feeling the tufted carpet pressing not ungently into her flesh. Wankel. Ah, Wankel! She did not know how it could be, but the floor was a hammock in which she and Wankel hung suspended between earth and air. Positive thinking; the tinsel flashed warningly at her, but she did not see it. Positive thinking; she sighed and swung and swung and sighed. That hair, that lip, that eye, that cheek!

But then, beyond the rhythmic creaking of the hammock rope, she heard the more substantial sound of footsteps on a stair, her stairs. Quick as a coursed hare she was out of the hammock and at the table where her work was laid out neatly waiting. Sex and Intellect. She groaned, trying to adjust the hair, the clothes, the mind, disturbed by hammock hands. And listening as the steps went past her door and into the room beyond, she put her head in her hands and said out loud, but quietly in case the lodger might hear, 'O God, why do you do it to me?'

Suzie woke to a curious hush. The light, coming into the bedroom nearly unobstructed by the cotton curtains (which she would have because darkness disturbed her), showed her it was quite late. Eight-thirty, perhaps more. But where was the traffic? Though the house was on a little-used side street, she could usually hear, long before dawn crawled in to put the street-lamps out, the heavy rumble of traffic on the arterial roads and the more distant clank of train wheels crossing the iron bridge. But this morning there was little sound, and what there was seemed muted to her listening ear.

And – even more strange – there was Larry, still lying in the bed beside her. She could see out of the corner of her eye the iridescence of his shocking pink pyjamas edging over the far corner of the sheet.

For though they inhabited, through custom rather than

preference, the same bed, they chose to occupy its extreme edges, putting as much distance between their two selves as possible. They each seemed to be afraid that the other harboured some grave infection, which the slightest contact of flesh would transmit.

Suzie had recently been wondering whether she should broach with Larry the question of separate beds. But something forbade it. Separate beds! – whispers from childhood keyholes. Separate beds! – low conversation through half-open doors. Separate beds had always seemed to Suzie a social disgrace only marginally less serious than leprosy.

So this morning, as every other morning for the past five years (and one or two before, never admitted) their two bodies were juxtaposed under a civilized covering of feather and down; but their two minds marauded outwards, quartering the colder regions of their individual separateness.

Suzie got out of bed very carefully, so that she could wrap around her the neck-to-feet protection of her woollen dressing gown, before Larry had the opportunity of seeing her half-bared flesh. She was not worried that the sight of it might give him what – in the language which had so permeated her childish self – was shudderingly referred to as 'ideas'. No, Larry had no 'ideas' about her, no designs on her unwilling person. She was as interesting to him as a neutered bitch. And gradually, gradually, as day mounted day and the weeks bred fast and fecund, in such a way had Suzie come to see herself.

So now she hurried into the concealing dressing gown with only a passing glance towards the mirror to check the progress of her mouth (no extra growth had recently occurred) and saw, through the space where the curtains were not drawn close, the reason for the unusual quiet.

Over the small patch of grass behind the house; over the dividing wall, the dustbin lids, the one tree clinging to existence by the narrow path; over the dingy roof of next-door's house, and the one beyond, and all those beyond and across and beside, tucked jowl to jowl, overlooking and overlooked, foundation locked into foundation, as close and painful as arthritic hands, over it all some saving spell had, during the night, been cast. Or so it seemed to Suzie, not yet totally awake and seeing through unjaundiced eye the fresh coating of snow which lay as lightly as plucked down over the city, softening and blurring with its thick-bristled brush until the whole seemed scarcely real, a toy town in a picture book.

Suzie looked at it with the first pure pleasure she had felt since Wankel's knee touched her knee. Wankel. She was seeing him today. At the thought all pleasure in the snowy scene dispersed, for how would she get to him with the city slowed, stopped – so it seemed to her from the lack of sound – and worse, far worse, Larry kept to the house, his presence, usually so forgettable, holding her there as effectively as if the house were a cell, and she secured in it by lock and key.

She heard the water gushing through the pipes as the lodger flushed the lavatory, and sent up an anguished plea to the god-she-did-not-believe-in to spare her a day of enforced proximity with the two people whose presence would disturb her most.

But her plea, reaching no sympathetic ear, fell into the abyss where unheard pleas must languish for eternity, and Larry stayed home and the lodger stayed home, and the snow was quickly tainted with the grey wash which hung like an ill-fitting skin over the city, just visible between the tower blocks and the sky.

And though the streets began to clear of it, and the traffic began to move, still the lodger and the husband sat and stayed. Suzie, retiring to her room to work, heard how the city was beginning to flow again, a great self-feeding river, and felt herself marooned, the space behind the green front door in which she was confined an island, increasingly isolated as the tide rose around it, she at its centre, an iris of silence and inactivity.

She tried to work. The deadline for her article on sex and intellect was approaching, and the editor of *Wag-On*, a large and formidable matron of twenty, was already rumbling *basso profundo* about drafts and copy dates.

The first section, 'The History of Sex' had been quite easy, a factual, informative preparation for the meat of the matter. She wondered whether she should have attempted a complementary 'History of Intellect' but there were so few female intellects to write the history of; and the editor had vetoed her suggestion of men. She had begun the second edition, 'Sex and the Relationship', a week before but had progressed only as far as the introductory sentence: 'A sexual relationship between adults should always be based on mutual respect and honesty'. Somehow, after that, inspiration had deserted her.

She sat, turning her pencil round and round in her hand, like the wild needle of a faulty compass, while her mind stayed obstinately blank. She stared in turn at the window, the wall, the floor, the page and back to the wall again. Her mind just then existed in a curious limbo, seeking forward to uncharted worlds like a spaceship on an outward voyage. The minute craters of the wall grew as if they were the craters of some alien planet, which as she drew near it, swelled until it occupied the whole span of her vision, a huge and vacant land.

And on to this she set, as the city came to life beyond the green front door unnoticed, unremembered, scenes that she desired, scenes of which she was afraid, scenes of reality and unreality, of success, failure and mortification, all drawn with the same dark brush of her half-loosened mind, uniformly sombre, with a curious transparent shadowyness, like the petals of a flower planted in unfriendly soil, denied sufficient light.

And so the morning passed without her knowing it, until the opening and closing of the green front door shuddered up through the masonry, the wood, the chair and into her bones, and she was brought back from her journey to the reality of Larry's back retreating down the street, of the empty page on which she had written not a word.

The woven images unravelled. The bright light, too real outside her window and magnified to a glare by the still-lying snow, drove out the last threads. Yet their shadow lingered with her, superimposed onto the substance of the city like a photographic negative; lurking just visible at the outer edges of her eyes, so that when she turned quickly she almost caught sight of – something; she was not sure what.

While she had been dreaming the city had come back to itself. The traffic was moving freely down the cleared streets, people were picking their way along the pavements, over piles of discoloured slush. And Larry had gone. Suzie breathed deeply, thankfully. The room seemed larger, as though the walls had taken a step back from her. As she got up and moved away from the desk, her whole body felt lighter, looser jointed. Larry had gone. She would see her poet. Wankel. Little darts of energy juddered the surface of her skin. Wankel. Her muscles emptied of lethargy, and she went across the landing and down the stairs with quick, lithe steps, like a dancer, like an athletic child.

Not even the lodger who came to the door of his room and watched her with the cold eye of an owl speculating at the moon, disturbed her. She was humming as she picked up the telephone; she was humming as she put it down. And the humming stayed with her, a small quivering set at the deep root of her tongue, a vibration high in the hollow of her nose, as she crossed the inelegance of the thawing city, and passed out of respectable suburbia into the dubious huddle of houses that was Lazarus Street.

If Suzie was honest with herself, she would have admitted that she did not want to meet her poet in Lazarus Street. Still more, not in the ungainly and forbidding church which topped the rise marking the very midpoint of the slum.

It is the sort of church which any day and with no notice given to the regular congregation of one, may be turned into a community centre. The kind of draughty, comfortless establishment where interlocking plastic chairs numb resting buttocks, and chilled hands may be held out to the slight warmth of a single paraffin stove. Where coffee is tuppence a cup, and do-gooding a penny. Where you may hear bad poetry any evening, bad advice all day.

But then, that day not so long ago when Suzie slid and stumbled up the rise to meet her Wankel, then church was

56

church. A notice on the rusty iron railings said 'No Trespassing'; and the door, sternly studded above the worn stone steps, was locked.

Suzie walked with difficulty through the drifts carved around the fume-grimed walls, seeking a side entrance. The grave stones reared up big and black above the white; and the white crust which sat astride this scroll, that angel's wing, was queerly incongruous, like an old woman dressed up in a younger woman's hat. Suzie saw, through the carved-out centre of a leaning cross, two young men kissing. She walked past them taking no notice, or trying not to. For despite her liberal views, this juxtaposition of male and male, of sex and death, disturbed her.

The disturbance followed her in through the side door of the church which by some accident was not locked. The door groaned as she pushed it inwards, echoing in her the childhood horror of horror – bats in belfries, vampires and phosphorescent hounds.

The church inside was very dim, the narrow windows obscured on the outside by a layer of grime, like an ancient dust-sheet cast over the roof and hanging down the walls, giving the gaunt Christ, nailed to the single stained-glass cross, a colouring so tainted that he might have been mistaken for black.

And Wankel, stepping out with unnecessary suddenness from behind a pale pillar, increased her disturbance. For where everything around was dim and dark, Wankel stood out pale, almost luminous, as if whatever light had seeped into the place was drawn into his flesh, and petrified there. He looked like stone itself, his flesh stone, his eyes stone cataracts stolen from some statue.

But the weird impression passed almost immediately, as he walked up to her standing stork-like in her spattered yellow wellingtons, watching him come, seeing how his nearly spontaneous smile curled back his lip to expose the crooked tooth, how his hands were pushed deep into his pockets in exaggerated casualness, how his trousers caked at the bottom with slush and mud just showed the outline of his thinnish calf, and hung not quite long enough above his leather ankle boots, like half-rigged storm sails.

Suzie said, 'Hello.'

So did Wankel, at exactly the same moment, one voice vying with the other, neither making itself heard; and both bouncing simultaneously but separately from pillar to wall to floor, the stone picking up the syllables and tossing them to and fro, leaving Wankel and Suzie standing foolish, not knowing quite what to do, two novice pigs-in-the-middle, uncertain of the rules, uncertain even of the game.

The gloom of the place and its musty decrepitude subdued the remnants of Suzie's pleasurable anticipation. She wanted to leave straightaway. She pushed her glasses up on her nose and opened her mouth, but shut it again without saying anything; for Wankel was stroking the halo of a mournful plaster virgin, looking intently into the empty middle-ground. Suzie hoped it was not a poem coming on. She did not feel up to a poem.

But no poem appeared. Wankel continued to stroke and stare, stroke and stare, until Suzie was quite unnerved by it, and jumped like a stung mare when he said suddenly, and without any alteration in look or stance, 'Quite a place, eh?'

Suzie peered at him. It was difficult to decipher detail in the gloom, but he looked serious.

'The atmosphere!' Wankel rolled his eyes at her. Suzie wondered briefly whether he was drunk, but could detect no hint of it on his breath. She wished he would not choose such an inappropriate time to be dramatic. Her feet were cold and she wanted a gin.

But Wankel was oblivious to it. He began to enumerate the dramatic virtues of the place, symbolic, he said, of darkness and death. His voice vibrated with only slightly feigned intensity as he demanded whether Suzie could not see this place as a latter-day Lazarus' tomb?

As if in response to some mysterious and unseen clue, a figure floated up out of the darker recesses by the font. Wankel stared fearfully at it, wondering whether he could possibly have invoked some risen representative of Christ the King. But it was only the vicar, wading forward through the dimness in a pair of wellingtons, his dark suit almost indistinguishable from the background shadows, his face, lined as a last-year's nut, seeming momentarily, to Wankel's inflamed imagination, like a beheaded ghost. But not even Wankel, though he tried, could translate the yard broom resting jauntily upon the clerical shoulder, into a symbol of the cross.

And as he came up to them they could see he was a little, ordinary man, rather shrivelled, as though he had approached too closely the glory of God, and suffered first degree burns. He looked from one to the other like a sparrow sizing up two rival bits of grain.

'Is it a wedding?' he said.

Then as Wankel cleared his throat and Suzie put her hand up to her mouth, he added with a sly grin, 'Oh, it's all right! We don't mind about divorce. Fresh start, mmm? That's what we believe in here; they don't call us St Lazarus' Church for nothing! Eh?'

Had he been standing nearer Suzie felt he would have nudged her with his elbow, an ungenteel meeting of bone on flesh. As it was, he satisfied himself with a quick smirk and a little jig on the spot, which caused his wellingtons to make a hollow, flapping sound against his legs, and sent small flurries of snow drifting off the clogged bristles of the broom. He reminded Suzie of the witch who had terrorized the pages of her childhood picture book. She muttered something vaguely negative and Wankel joined in.

'Not a wedding? Pity; pity. We do such lovely weddings here. My own dear wife and I were joined before this very altar. Marvellous woman; blessing for the parish. What she can do with the Widows and Orphans! Ah – not a funeral?'

'No; no.'

Wankel and Suzie spoke in unison now as if the presence of the vicar had moulded together their tongues into one imperfect harmony. The vicar looked puzzled and scratched the side of his nose with a dry forefinger before saying cautiously, 'Er – baptism?'

Receiving no immediate negative response he went on hurriedly, as if it were a business deal which a little adept persuasion could clinch, 'We welcome anyone, anyone at all to our flock. Sheep of all ages and, er' (here peering closely at Wankel) 'and, er, types. No?'

Wankel and Suzie both shook their heads in tandem, twin puppets whose single string seemed to be attached to the jerky bobbing of the vicar's shaven chin.

'Well,' he said, wagging his finger at them and maintaining with an effort his jocularity (for baptisms, brides and burials are the meat of the cleric's profession) – 'if it's confession you're after, you'll have to call on those other lot, you know, the opposition! Ah – ha – ha.'

Suzie drew a shape on the flagstone with the toe of her yellow wellington and said into the silence which disdained the vicar's clumsy humour, 'We were just looking, actually.'

The vicar swung his broom off his shoulder and leaned his weight onto it, as if he had suddenly found he needed support. 'Looking? Just Looking?'

He looked about him, ceiling, walls, floor, as if in an attempt to confound the very notion of 'looking'. His neck was strangely supple so that he could twist his head on it so far round that he resembled an ageing parrot surveying some intruder from the safety of his perch.

'My dear young lady,' he said looking at Suzie in mock severity, adopting that patronizing tone peculiar to men of the cloth who disapprove of young and flighty women, 'My dear young lady. You cannot "just look" in here. This is a church, not a chainstore.'

Wankel, who had moved away as if by the simple act of creating physical distance between them he could dissociate himself entirely, circled back and hissed at Suzie from the safety of a pillar, 'Don't argue with him. Let's go.'

Suzie, who was already retreating before the vicar's 'now if you two good people will excuse me', and general shooing motions, which he emphasized by the thrusting forward of the broom, felt aggrieved. For the meeting in the church had been

Wankel's suggestion. It had been the only place he could think of, the pubs being shut, where the one could wait for the other in some kind of protection from the weather.

For though Lazarus Street is a street of doorways and alleys and little set-back pieces just big enough for a body to conceal itself in, no self-respecting body will linger more than a minute. For Lazarus Street is the no-man's land between tight little terraces of urban respectability (such as is contained behind Suzie's green front door) and the sprawling pseudo-Bohemian lairs into which can be tracked university students, poets, musicians, out-of-work artists and an abundance of bankrupt stock. And into this no-man's land as into a vacuum are sucked the least desirable elements of society: blacks, prostitutes, second-rate clerics, winos, vagrants, estate agents, pimps, buskers, documentary film-makers, exploiters and exploited, all sucked in on the wind which scours the littered pavements, throws into the air old newspaper, a hat, a dead leaf or a graveside prayer, each with the same lack of discrimination, a god-like disinterestedness, with which it now takes the side door of Saint Lazarus' church and slams it shut behind the Wankel and the Suzie who stop beside a monument while the same wind tugs at their clothes, as if it is trying to move them out of there, out of that inadequate protection provided by the rusty railings of sanctity, into the total exposure of the street.

Wankel said, 'What a character!' and swiftly made notes in his leather-bound notebook. But they must have been very brief notes, for almost at once he closed the book and put it away, drawing his gloves thankfully over chilled fingers.

Suzie said, 'I'm cold.'

So Wankel, always gallant as long as it did not inconvenience him, offered her his scarf, which she wound round and round her neck until it circled out nearly as far as the edges of her narrow shoulders, like a wrongly-placed life belt, from whose centre her head poked up, small and incongruous as a crocus through snow.

They walked round to the front of the church, and out through the gate. In the street some children were throwing snowballs, rival gangs who plotted and giggled and swore and screamed with feigned rage when a handful of wet snow landed on their necks and melted coldly under their collars. Beyond them the two young men who had been kissing by the gravestone were walking away hand in hand. Suzie peered after them thinking she saw something familiar in the shape of the one. But a near miss had sprayed her glasses with flakes of ice, and her sight was blurred.

She took off her glasses to wipe them, and while she was in that half-blind and vulnerable state there came, sudden, unexpected over the high mirth of the children, the sound of glass shattering. It became very quiet, very quickly. Suzie put on her glasses and saw that everyone was still, and staring upwards. She stared too, and saw that Christ was falling from his stained glass cross, his crown of thorns broken away, his hands stretched out seekingly on either side, as he somersaulted slowly to the ground and shattered into tiny pieces on the top step of the church, outside the locked and studded doors.

Everything was quiet while the echoes of disintegration washed along the street like little tidal waves, lapped against the feet of Suzie, who believed in none of it, yet to whom the destruction of an idol was, in a vague and terrible way, portentous.

Then as Wankel crossed himself surreptitiously and reached for his notebook, a howl rose up from the watchers, a shriek of pure pagan joy, as at the ritual destruction of some alien god; and they rushed through the iron gate and up the steps, pushing Suzie and Wankel aside, to retrieve a sliver of glass, part of the crown, an eye, anything, their share in this moment of triumph.

Wankel said, rather fearful, 'Come on. Let's go. You've seen enough.'

But Suzie was not looking at the children or the glass or the gaping window. She was watching instead how the two young men had stopped by the low wall of a partly-demolished house, and one was flexing his right arm, holding it out in front of him and stretching the fingers, as if the arm had just been used for some swift physical movement, such as the throwing of a stone.

And as they grinned and looked into each other's eyes, and began to turn away from her, Suzie was almost sure, though at that moment a newspaper blew up obscuring her view, that one of them was Rex.

Suzie gazed into Wankel's eyes and said, 'They're big.'

Wankel smiled in modest self-dismissal and said, 'Well; not really. Other people's are just as big.'

'Oh, no; I don't think so.'

Suzie was stroking with her forefinger the bare skin of Wankel's biceps. The way the flesh fluttered under her touch fascinated her, but at the same time was oddly repellent. She remembered how she had once stroked a nestful of naked birds like this, with the very end of her finger, and how they had shifted and mewed under her touch. The next day she had found them beheaded by a fox, spread bloody and pitiful on the ground, their wings wide, transparent, like tiny white bats.

Suzie did not think that Wankel's biceps were the biggest she had ever seen. She had not made sufficient study of biceps to be able to compare. Biceps, to tell the truth, bored her. She preferred mind to muscle and had flattered Wankel only because, as all sagacious women know, men must be flattered.

For if men are not flattered, how will the world go round? Newton would surely never have discovered Gravity without a good woman flatteringly behind him. Einstein's Relativity would have been lost to us forever had not some woman, somewhere, fondled some part of his anatomy (possibly his head) and simpered, 'Ooh; isn't it big?'

Thus, Suzie reclining on Wankel's second-hand goatskin rug, warmed by the single bar of his electric fire, wondering what should happen next, wondering which move she should make to be right, as though there were some set of rules governing such dalliance which must strictly be adhered to, or the game is lost.

Wankel, with his chest partly uncovered and fondling with one hand a Suzie thigh, was lamenting the waywardness of flesh. But this time it was his own which troubled him. For where there should have been life, there was none. The desire which he was sure he felt, remained contained within his head. His limp responses were becoming an embarrassment.

And it was not as if Suzie were undesirable. She was remarkable, for a woman of thirty-three. Only the merest hint of slackness at the neck; belly still firm (as far as he could see, held in as it was by the close material of her jeans); and no hint of that baggyness about the upper arm which quite revolted him.

And the time was undoubtedly right. He had abstained from flesh, real or imagined, for several days. He had been careful in his diet, abstemious in his alcohol. His bowel movements were regular. What more propitious time could there be?

Yet still his mind steered itself away from the task in hand. He remembered, though he did not want to, the last time he had entertained upon this very rug, real flesh. It had been after the Literary Comrades Annual General Meeting, where various stirring resolutions had been passed which were certain to bring art to the people; (or was it the people to art? Wankel could not quite recall. He had been contemplating at the time the dimpled kneecap of the wife of the Comrade Chairman, a delectable little piece whose 'Power to the People' sash rose and fell so delightfully over her young, moulded bosom, that Wankel thought it could easily have been replaced by 'Miss World' or even 'Miss Universe'). And Wankel had narrowly missed being voted in as the People's Arts Officer. Whether it was euphoria at the success of the resolutions, or relief at his failure to be elected, is uncertain, but some strong swelling of emotion had caused Wankel to invite to his rooms a certain community artist, a young lady of obvious charm and intelligence, who exhorted her comrades from the platform to 'butcher the Imperialist Pigs and set the People free'. Wankel had been enchanted. But his enchantment had not survived their sojourn on the goatskin rug, where the lady had stripped to reveal a body entirely covered with People's Party slogans, and had questioned him closely, as she removed with the deft fingers of a surgical nurse, shirt, trousers, thermal underwear (it had been a cold day), on his commitment to the theories of Lenin.

He remembered now with a shudder which he could not

suppress, how, eyeing in turn his collection of Bach and his absence of physical response, she had got up, dressed, and left on the tide of something which sounded like 'bourgeois fool'; or had it been 'bourgeois tool'?

Suzie, on whom the draught which sneaked in under the ill-fitting door was causing goose-flesh, felt the shudder as it rippled down to the tips of Wankel's fingers, and said, 'Is anything the matter?'

Wankel said, 'No; no,' and wished that it were true. For he was beginning to be concerned by the obstinacy of his flesh, which remained immune to all of Suzie's obvious enticements, too many to enumerate, but amongst which the chief two were that she was female and available. Could it be, wondered Wankel, that the community artist – and the taste of failure – were coming between them? He thought not, for what was one small failure when he was Wankel? Then could it be . . . As he ran his hand down Suzie's denimed thigh he was conscious of a slight distaste, a sour coating on his tongue.

He thought how different it would be if she had on a skirt. He imagined the fall of the material away from the hip; the manoeuvrability of cloth on flesh; the way the lower thigh, sheened by its nylon covering, would disappear into the mysterious darkness of petticoat, and stocking top, and smooth warm skin.

Lace; the resistance, the suppleness, of lycra and elastic; incomprehensible fastenings; the little ridges of constriction in the skin; hooks, eyes, bows, panels of satin; ah . . .!

Suzie, quite cold and uncomfortable, submitted to Wankel's exploratory hands much as she might have to a doctor's, on the greater comfort of the examination table; and watched, meanwhile, the circle swum by Wankel's goldfish, a gift from his youngest child who had won it at a fair. She watched how it swam round and round and round, always seeking outwards but contained behind the glass, eyes round, mouth an oscillating circle which, with a little alchemy, might easily expand to take in and consume the universe.

She looked at Wankel and saw his mouth as the same dark

65

maw but uncontained and predatory. And the darkness of it seemed to her the darkness of the unknown, the unimagined. She thought she could see no end to the darkness there; it was some terrible infinity in which all horrors could, in due time, be discovered; but which was now filled entirely with emptiness, so complete it seemed to her that it could only be death.

And as she looked the darkness spread out from him and the hands which he moved on her body seemed to dissolve, the flesh of them melting and falling off the bone, until only the bone was left, very white, very dry, a skeleton which scratched inquisitively around her body's boundaries.

Wankel said, 'The zip; er – can you help?'

He was tugging ineffectually with his long, white fingers at the zipper of her jeans, whose teeth had caught up the material and held it fast. Suzie said, 'No!' and sat up very quickly, so quickly that she quite put Wankel off balance and he collapsed clumsily onto one shoulder. 'No; I must go; the time . . . .'

She pulled her sweater down decisively around her hips, and reached for her shoes. The vision had left her but the taste of it remained. She avoided looking at Wankel's hands.

While Suzie fussed and tidied and adjusted in a fretful, random way, as though her mind were half elsewhere, Wankel lay on his back tracing the cracks in the ceiling and trying to steady his breathing. Flesh was wholly incomprehensible; his; theirs; all of it. It would be better if flesh were peeled from bone, no flesh existed, and human beings were merely motivated skeletons. He thought he would give it up, devote himself completely to his Art. And Suzie! He would certainly abandon her; she was wayward, perverse, too trousered.

Yet as she got up and he saw how her buttocks mounded out so firm and round above the thigh, he wondered whether he might not relent. She certainly was a remarkable woman for thirty-three. And next time – next time – perhaps she might even wear a skirt.

Wankel is dreaming. From a long way off he hears his mother's voice. He cannot tell at first what she is saying and wonders, in the curiously detached manner of dreamers, whether she is at last dead, and speaking to him from the great beyond. Not that he usually believes in a beyond, although he accedes in public to the popular notion that hell is created here on earth, by people like himself. But sleep lifts off the mind's veneers and sometimes in his dreams he comes to perceive, if not a heaven or a hell, then at least an identifiable something. And that something is more comfortable than the great darkness of eternal oblivion. For Wankel, and his ego, find morality hard to accept.

But what his mother is saying when he at last manages to decipher word from word, seems quite unlike a spirit message, or at least Wankel's untutored belief as to what such a message should be.

'What?' he says, and 'what?' struggling through the mists which clog and crystallize inside his brain.

'Are you comin' home fer Christmas, Son?'

Each word reverberates through him like a struck bell.

'I'm goin' to decorate. Tinsel, an' a tree. Are you comin'?'

He hears as though she is in the room with him the click of her dentures settling back onto her jaw, imagines how the loose skin hangs in wattles between neck and jaw. His mother is old. If she is not dead yet – and he is now nearly certain it is not a spirit voice which talks to him – she will soon die. In she who begat him is proof of a mortality which will cull him as surely, if not as swiftly, as it will cull her.

This dream – if dream it is – begins to apportion to itself the horrors of a nightmare. Is she there? Is she not there? And he, where is he? For if, hearing her voice so clearly he can doubt the existence of his mother, why should he not doubt his own, for which he has no proof except the vague and shifting currents forming his thoughts? And might it not be possible for thoughts to exist apart from things? Apart from flesh, self personality? Possibilities ravel up his brain like so much shrunken cloth. There is no end to its convolutions.

But gradually the image of his mother – her voice, her teeth – fades, and into the space left by the departed dream there floats a perfect sphere of peace; white, round as a blank balloon. How long it hangs, a limbo in his brain, he cannot tell. But soon, too soon, on to its anonymity his thoughts inscribe outlines, faces of women and of wives; of memories, and regrets. They all pass through him like a carnival procession of clowns. He can remember them so clearly in his dream, more clearly than in reality, as if they were a counterpoint to his unconsciousness. This one, fair hair snaking down her back like liquid light. That one whose eyes, green and opaque as leaves, stare through him unrecallingly. This one, whose teeth show small and even when she draws back her narrow lip. That one, a blemish brushed onto the base of her spine like ochre paint, which carves in him a niche so sure that when he wakes he is surprised to find himself unblemished.

And last of all in the procession comes Suzie. Clearer even than the rest, because more recent. Clearer too because she is at least in part imagined not remembered. For she is as yet mysterious, with the mystery Wankel knows to be possessed only by women; that mystery of their different selves; that dark, guarded, secret otherness to which as man he has no access. A witch's brew whose composition can be only guessed at. Eye of newt, toe of frog. . . . It is a power which fascinates him, of which he is afraid. It is the element which draws him towards women like an unseen thread, always towards them, always afraid that it will snare him.

He has sought this mystery in them all. Sometimes he has been so near that he has felt its shape, traced with his mind's finger the unfamiliar outline. But always when he has taken hold of it, it has dispersed as surely as a reached mirage. And he has come away frustrated, cheated, as if the grail had been snatched out of his hands. Yet still they accuse him, in his dream. For though he has gained nothing, yet in some strange contradictory way, the women have lost all.

But what and how he does not know. Perhaps, perhaps the answer lies in Suzie. Suzie, still whole where the others are husked. Suzie, who remains while he disperses them with the exhalation of a breath. She is to him just now as precious as a sealed cask, whose treasures may outshine the gold of Tutankhamun. So Wankel, for a while, dreams.

But as the dream grows and changes, so Suzie alters. Nothing, at first, no more than a blurring of feature, a change of colour or curve. It occurs so gradually that he wonders whether he will ever know who she is changing into. Then quite suddenly, as though a signal had been given and received, the image he has created comes into focus, so clearly he can see the graining of the skin, the wrinkling of the drab flesh at the corner of the mouth, as the mouth opens and his mother says, 'Don't you worry about me, Son; don't you worry about your mother.'

Wankel tries to scream but in the way dreams are, uncontrollable, perverse, he cannot. And his scream in any case is stopped somewhere in his throat, for there is more to come.

As he contemplates the grotesque outline of his mother in Suzie's underwear (so far had his dreams of her progressed) the image alters yet again. The hands which touch and stroke the garments – lace, lycra, and queer silky stuff which causes pleasurable shivers to run through him – grow and coarsen. The body too thickens and changes shape. The legs, inside their shiny stockinged case, are muscled and sinewy. Wankel stares. And his attention seeking upwards, past the manly muscle of abdomen, the broad chest, the heavy shoulder, up the curiously narrow neck, discovers the face; his face.

Wankel stares at Wankel; grey eye contemplates grey eye. The Wankel image seems to be at once both guilty and defiant. There is no lowering of the glance in shame, no modest covering of the body with the hands. Wankel is shocked, but something else, something more. . . .

For as he watches the Wankel-image he imagines how those things would feel next to his own flesh, the taut constriction of bra and suspender belt, the scratchy unfamiliarity of lace edging; the give of straps and panels as his body moves. And above all, the silken (oh, so sensual!) caress of the stockings. So clearly does Wankel experience their texture and their strangely alien scent that it is almost as if he himself were so dressed.

And as the music strikes up somewhere, a band, with the

familiar raucous strain, *da* da da; da *da* da da, he gradually becomes aware as garment follows garment into the darkness which is filled now with whistles and shouts and cries and stamps – he gradually becomes aware that he is not watching, but doing. Wankel is Wankel. Dream and dreamer fuse as completely and inextricably as sperm meeting ovum. And from that fusion grows a strange triumph; for it is as if the answer to the mystery he has so long sought to solve has been discovered within himself. He is an indestructible circle of self conjoined with self; he has no need either to admit or transmit; not to possess, but to be; for Wankel, in his dream, is woman.

And everything is light and noise and colour and good. The crowd, devouring him, roars and sighs; only the final fragment of cloth, and he is theirs. But at that moment of triumph, the scene is split by the clamouring of a bell. The ambulance; the police; death; destruction; guilt; all swamp him like a noxious tidal wave on whose crest he rises and wakes to the darkness of his bed, his room, thick and stultifying, the restriction of his own flesh, and through it all the insistent summons of bell, bell, bell.

He stumbles through the bedroom door, out of the heavy darkness of his room into the pale illumination of street light through thin curtaining. The telephone is cool and hard to his touch, too real. Fumbling, he puts it to his ear. From a long way off, as if she is standing at the furthest shore-line of his mind, he hears his mother saying to him, 'Are you comin' home fer Christmas, Son?'

4

If I knew where the beginning was, I would begin there. For today, which is a cold, bored sort of day, I am in the mood for contemplation. My poet is away on a trip; likewise my Larry. Two antipathetic arrows, one travelling North, one South; one by plane, one by train. I would like to think of myself as the motivating bow which has propelled them out on their distinct trajectories. But women are such passive creatures, we are told, capable of catalytic influence only. Very well. I stay at home and work my alchemy. While the men go North, go South, go, do, be, become, I – contemplate.

But still, despite my alchemy, despite my all, I do not know where to begin. And beginnings are important, for in them can often be discerned the shape of endings. What use are endings? They are important only in as much as they can help to place the present. For women – and I am no exception – want to know where they are.

'Oh yes, I went back to him', says the wife of a vicious rapist; 'We talked it over; it's all right, now we know where we are'.

'No, I'm going to stay with him', says the woman of the man who beats her regularly twice a week. 'At least I know him; at least I know where I am'.

But I, on the contrary, am uncertain just now as to where I am. Or perhaps I should say where we are, for my uncertainty centres around my poet. Although I am coming increasingly to know the man – that he is a creature of socks and handkerchiefs and ill-assorted ties; that he frets over food, farts quietly in corners and walks away – yet I am coming less and less to know the situation. For intention has not been followed by consummation; desire has not been fulfilled. Each meeting is anticipated with increasing ardour. Increasingly more time is spent on the imagination of face, voice, accidental touch. Yet the reality is stilted; meetings contrived at furtive little country pubs; low-voiced, awkward conversations mirrored in the shallow shine of last week's horse brass; dry fingers briefly met over a plastic table top; and a few fumbling explorations in the front seat of the car, hampered by gear sticks, hand brakes, imitation sheepskin seat covers and vinyl fascia boards with little lights that wink at you obscenely, knowingly.

I feel something should occur, or we will tire of it. And I, my poet and our promising diversion, will be relegated to the annals of what might have been. I do not believe in might-have-beens; might-have-beens belong to languishing and Lilians. A Lil can, with a little wit, translate might into is.

Brave words; but still I am seeking – no solution, only a beginning. And it is difficult to decide where such beginnings are. Where is the birth of the affair?

The first meeting? The first eye-contact which has shed indifference and with it stripped away that thin outer layer of the mind – its innocence? The first anticipatory whisper of flesh on flesh? The first covert suggestion, the first overt? The first illicit meeting? The first fuck?

Or does the beginning belong elsewhere? In a disaffection, a sudden realization of the perfunctory nature of the goodbye kiss, the familiar fondle which provokes not passion but a yawn? The discovery that he talks too little or too much or fails to flush the lavatory?

Or is it earlier than that, somewhere on the path to discovering who you are, some incident of man or men or self which shuts off like points closing a railway track the set of possibilities which would have stamped 'fidelity' all through you like a stick of rock?

Or earlier even than that, long, long, before the lisping on a Daddy's knee of the refrain, Lil is a good girl, good girl, good. . . . Before all that, back to the first fusion of existence, sperm and ovum clasped in the passionless embrace beginning life. Is the affair within you even then, locked in a mysterious genetic heritage, inhabiting the Pandora's box of the pre-socialized self, until one day, wandering the maze of doors you open one unknowingly, and – smoke from a Genie's lamp – the essence of the affair sneaks out?

Oh, Fidelity! As long as you both shall live, says the vicar, relishing behind his cassock and his lifted ring yesterday's choirboy, last year's whore. As long as we both shall live, think the bride and groom, temporarily blinded by the sudden abundance of unproscribed genital. As long as we both shall live, thinks the rejected husband, as he eyes the implacable fortress of his wife's turned shoulder; thinks the woman preparing to endure with an assumed complaisance some male weight of muscle and bone, while already contemplating tomorrow's pork chop, next week's bills.

Oh, Infidelity! Synonymous, perhaps, only with opportunity, reflowering of that which has been pressed dry between marital sheets; an oasis set in an aridity. A whole capsule of stimulants far outweighing any that can be acquired by a doctor's note. All the costly rejuvenating powders, potions, oils, remedies – all compressed into the essence of a single touch, a look.

See that woman there who moves her body down the street exuding the allure made legendary by Mata Hari? She is having an affair. Or that one who, last week, her face in its habitual repose of discontent looked faded, used; now she is filled with animation, extending out to every nerve and sinew, out even into the air surrounding her, so that she exists in a cocoon of it, and is, for this moment, almost ageless; she too is having an affair.

But what of those, that couple who sit in the corner with the lights turned high, where everything is shown too clearly and the whole assumes the same stark, arid quality as a desert? Whose faces might be cut from paper, sketched with chalk on to a vacant board; whose eyes stare each through each unfocusing; to each of whom the other has become a blur, a mere amalgamation of cell and tissue, once desired, now barely noticed except as an encumbrance. Each mind has sloughed the other

73

off from it like a scab under whose covering new skin has grown, a cataract of separation. These two are faithful: thirty years; forty; cleaving to no one; warming their dry bones on fidelity.

I think I prefer being Lil.

For there is something pleasing in the way bad men come after you when you are Lil, in a way they would never contemplate, were you Lilian, or Lily. And good men, as all knowledgeable women will agree, are bores.

And so my bad man, my poet, my less-than-final-fling, my contemplation. If I knew where the beginning was, I would begin there. I would begin.

Oh Lil, I had forgotten how innately bad you are! Likeable, but bad. Just as some people are born with a hare lip, without arms, so you were born with your badness. I think it stems from the fact that you are possessed of dual genitalia, one set of which is in your head.

Two! One set is problematical enough, always wanting what you do not want, moving you to places you would rather not go. I think a woman would be better off without even the one.

For men it is not the same; a man could have two and never know the difference. For a man and his sexuality move in the same general direction; there is a compatibility between his physical and mental self. But for a woman, sex and intellect are mutually exclusive. The following of one means the abandonment of the other. Always there is the struggle for power between the two.

Few women are aware of it. You, Lil, sensing it sometimes like a finger laid lightly on a shoulder, have never articulated the idea. But I am wiser than you. I know and have always known.

Men do not know of it. Even my man, he who is not my husband, he does not know. I would tell you his name, but he has no name. He is Darling, the shield behind which we both can hide, never knowing what person each one is. In saying 'Darling' I say nothing; in responding he responds to nothing.

Though there are times when I think he would like to have a name, when he seeks it in my eyes, the darkness of which he tries to penetrate but cannot; for that darkness is nothing but the thin shadow cast between birth and death.

*

Suzie was feeling paranoid. She had been unsure what was the matter with her, uncertain where to place the blame for her general malaise. But having consulted her *Home Doctor*, which told her it was psychological, she went to the library to find out more.

The library, she nearly admitted to herself, was an excuse for avoiding confrontation with her article. She had fixed up a curtain in the bedroom which, when drawn, completely hid her desk. In this way she could avoid the start of guilt which jogged uncomfortably through her whenever she caught sight of the chair in which she should have been sitting, the written sheets which should by now have been forming a comfortable pile, but whose bulk barely disturbed the smooth line of the wooden top. She had missed the last WAG meeting and was nervous every time the telephone rang: perhaps it was the Chairperson chasing her. It was not precisely that she was afraid; but nor was she precisely unafraid. Nothing about Suzie was, just then, at all precise. Not her thoughts, which she was finding harder than ever to control; not her person which was coming to look in general rather ruffled, as though she were about to moult.

Nothing about her was precise. She fluttered from one thing to another, intending everything, achieving nothing. She wondered whether she might not be in love, but had forgotten, in detail, the symptoms, and could find no entry for it in her *Home Doctor*. And love was something which she did not really hold with nowadays; she was too old; paranoia was preferable.

So she went, huddled untidily inside her second best duffle coat, to the Central Library. It was not a pleasant journey; her ailment (if such it could be called) was worse.

For, from the moment she stepped outside the green front door and heard the safe snap of the lock behind her, she felt followed; yet she knew it could not be so. When she stopped and looked over her shoulder, which she tried not to do too often, since it was merely psychological, no one was there. Or, rather, many people were there, crossing roads, hurrying in and out of shops, stumbling, yelling, waving, frowning, all going about their normal business, none of whom seemed to be the least interested in her. Yet still, she felt as though she were being followed; there was a shadow of discomfort on her senses.

It had been there ever since she saw – or thought she saw – her lodger by St Lazarus Church. She had meant, when she got home that night, to challenge him, ask directly whether he had been there. But the afternoon with Wankel had disturbed her. The image of fleshless hands outweighed the problem of a fallen Christ.

But still she wondered and watched him covertly, as he went silently about the house, so silent and unobtrusive that his very absence from a room shouted the consciousness of his potential presence. She could discover nothing. He was entirely contained and watched her, in his turn, with a strange contempt just recognizable beyond the careful barrier of his neutrality.

She disliked him. His – what she classified in her head as 'deviance' – disturbed her. Not that she objected to queers as such. Anybody had a right to be queer; it was a free country; she was a liberal-minded human being. But the thought of him, separated from her by mere inches of ageing brick, carrying on perhaps, unheard of, unthought of practices – perhaps he even invited friends there, when she was out. The thought of it revolted her.

But there was more than that. He had been – must have been – following her. There was no other explanation. For since the day of the fallen Christ, Suzie had several times visited Lazarus Street and stood at the edge of the pavement opposite the steps, and looked at the top step from which all trace of glass had been removed, and looked at how the upper section of the window was covered in with corrugated iron, below which poked the naked ankles of the Christ – all that was left.

She did not know why she went there. It was, perhaps, symbolic; she was not sure of what. But that certain time of day when the winter afternoon is tilting towards night, attracted her there. And it was there, each time as the shadows were beginning to thicken and battalions of street lights take them on, that she could see her lodger; sometimes with a friend, sometimes alone. But each time coming there quite suddenly, so that she could not tell from which direction he had come. She knew that he saw her, though he made no sign. And she, wondering what he was doing there, where he would go next, reluctant to speak to him, hurried away and home by the shortest route.

And each time he was home before her; she did not know how it could be and puzzled over it into the night while Larry slept and snored. The lodger never mentioned seeing her; but when he looked at her there was a kind of recognition. And the next time, it would happen again.

So Suzie thought, he must be following her. Could he perhaps have been hired by Larry to spy? So much cheaper than a private detective; so much easier to watch her closely. She had watched Larry closely for a while to see if she could see some revelatory change in his behaviour, some hint or word or action that might suggest he suspected. But it was rather difficult, since watching him disturbed her, she was so unaccustomed to it, and besides it was a bore. In any case, he rarely spoke to her, and the only things he did when they were together were sleeping and reading. Still, she had not caught him in so much as an extraordinary look. She began to wonder whether she could have mistaken the whole. Had she really seen the lodger? Had she been to Lazarus Street at all? She reached for the *Home Doctor*, and diagnosed paranoia.

And now, on the way to the library, she began to be worried. Concealing on the one hand her mouth (which, though it had not grown significantly, still seemed to her to have spread so widely on her face that, if she did not conceal and control it, someone would notice) and on the other resisting with difficulty the urge to look over her shoulder, she huddled herself in through the tall revolving doors.

In the foyer, set on a metal plinth which sprouted like a smelted phallus from the grey stone floor, was a statue. At least, Suzie supposed it was a statue. It was so wholly neutral that, in other circumstances, it might have been a coat stand. Suzie edged closer to it wondering whether it might be a coat stand, for if so she would have liked to make use of it. Her coat was thick, the heating high. But just in time, as she was beginning to believe it was what it appeared, she saw a metal plaque pinned to the side which said, 'Holocaust'. And from behind it, as though at some sly signal, came a security guard.

'What a thing, eh?' he said, indicating with a familiar jerk of his head the work of art. 'Load o' rubbish, I call it; and the council gave a thousand for it. Ratepayers' money! I ask you. Looks like a bloomin' coat hanger to me.' He sniffed contemptuously and wiped his nose on the back of his hand.

Suzie stepped away from him and said, 'Oh; I don't know.'

The man grinned at her, showing victorious teeth. 'Ah! You just about got it there! Nor does anyone else! Handbag, dear.'

Suzie stared past him while he rummaged through her handbag, feeling vaguely molested. She did not like the way his short, thick fingers sorted through her things. And such searches always made her feel guilty, as though she had something to hide. Perhaps that was just another symptom of her paranoia.

On the other side of the barrier she adjusted her glasses and began to read the printed directions which took up nearly the whole of a large notice board. Libraries, she thought, were like obstacle races; numerous fences between you and your goal, each one a little different to test the strength and temper of your ingenuity. She would have asked someone, but she did not want to place herself and her mouth open to an inspection by the two girls at the Enquiries Desk, whom she had already seen nudge each other and look towards her. And who were in any case much too young, attractive and confident to be approachable.

So Suzie waded her way through the directions, along the narrow aisles, and eventually found 'Paranoia' huddled in the farthest corner, as though it were afraid of being discovered. And the people browsing there did so furtively, as though they were afraid of being discovered. Suzie, insinuating her slight body between two separate shelves, found herself next to a small man in a large round hat, who kept his hat pulled low down over his eyes, and muttered into the pages of a book, held close into his face.

As she squeezed past him he moved the book down a fraction

and hissed, 'Don't tell them I'm here; whatever you do, don't tell them!'

Suzie pushed up her glasses and whispered back, 'Er, no; all right; I won't,' and escaped gratefully into an empty reading booth.

She became engrossed in definitions, symptoms, diagnoses, cures, all of which increased her apprehension. She was certainly paranoid. Her symptoms were described exactly: her suspicion and mistrust of others; her feeling of being followed. Delusions of grandeur did not quite fit in – unless – was it, could it be that her castle was such a delusion? Her castle, for which she had planned and saved and studied and dreamed? And that picture which she cherished to herself, of her person, the very Lilian Suzie Highman (probably at least an Honourable by then) standing on the parapet and surveying the formal gardens and the meadow beyond the ha-ha where her sheep safely grazed? Was it no more than a wild dream to be clinically defined, dismissed, buried in the communal grave delusion, there to lie unmarked, unmourned?

She could not dwell on so painful an idea. That she was shaken by it could be seen in the way she pushed her glasses high onto the bridge of her nose, pushed her hair behind her ears, brought it forward again, fluttered her hands together and apart like weak small birds; stared at the page, the wall and the booth, which all blurred in together unrecognizably, seeing in a moment through them what five hundred years would find hard to accomplish: her castle's destruction.

Then beyond the crumbling battlements, beyond the semi-soundproofed doorway of the booth, she heard a sudden commotion which brought her back to the reality of library, book and self. She looked up and saw through the wired glass which formed the centre panel of the door, the little man. His large round hat was missing, and the book behind which he had so carefully hidden. His hair was sticking out above his ears untidily, as though he had stood out somewhere in a high wind; and on either side of him, each with a firm hold on his arm, were two men in uniform.

The little man was behaving quite as wildly as his hair; he jigged about on the spot like a marionette; Suzie almost expected to see the strings which worked him. As he caught sight of her he became distraught and cried, 'You told them! You told them I was here!' And before Suzie could reply, the men in uniform hustled him away.

Suzie suddenly felt very tired, very confused. Everything was so difficult to decipher. What had the small man done? She closed the book and left the booth.

Putting the book back on the shelf she thought she saw, several aisles away and framed by the retreating spaces one behind the other into the perspective of a tunnel, the small man complete again with hat and book. But she knew it was not possible. She had seen him with her own eyes taken away; there surely could not be another just the same.

She was not aware of having spoken aloud, but as she passed out of 'Paranoia', several people turned and 'shushed' her angrily. It was a relief to find herself in 'Poetry', which was the section adjoining 'Paranoia' and a little smaller. Presumably, thought Suzie, there was more demand for 'Paranoia'; 'Poetry' was unvisited, other than by herself.

She looked along the shelves, idly, noticing names she knew, names which were unfamiliar to her. Then as though she were a ridden mare suddenly pulled up, she saw at the very end of the bottom shelf, tucked unobtrusively into the corner, but as obvious to her as if it had been garlanded with flashing lights, a slim dark volume on whose spine was inscribed in white the single word 'Wankel'.

At first she stared at it, afraid to pick it up. For, strange but true, she had never read a word of Wankel's work, not even the book he had given her. He had read aloud to her, sitting on a park bench crisped with cold, his words clouding out white into the air, like the balloons which hang above a cartoon character, meaningless until his creator enters something there. But she herself had never read a line. She had meant to, but when the moment came, she had avoided it as fastidiously as she might have avoided sorting through his exposed intestines with her bare fingers.

But now here was her poet, or a certain manifestation of him. Had she been someone else, a stronger person, more resolute, no doubt she would have vanquished temptation, passed the book by. But our Suzie can be nothing but herself, uncertain of that though she is. And were she strong and resolute she would not be our Suzie, Wankel's Suzie, Larry's Suzie, but some other, and belong elsewhere.

Our Suzie belongs irresolute, weak, shuddering with a strange, furtive apprehension among the shelves of 'Poetry', picking up as gingerly as though it were an explosive device, the thin dark volume with the legend 'Wankel' as indelibly upon the cover as it is upon her mind.

But though she picked the book up, opened it and saw the carefully set out pages of type, titles, stanzas, notes and acknowledgements, they meant nothing to her. For the first thing she had seen was Wankel, his photograph, ridiculously out of date, much younger, less grey altogether and more fleshed, but still with the unmistakable Wankel expression, that touch of self-satisfaction, as if he were patronizing the reader by the very act of appearing on the page. It had a peculiar effect on her; it raised not passion but compassion. Just then she was probably as open to the idea of Wankel, as vulnerable, as she would ever be. It was lucky he was not there to see and take advantage of it. But compassion is in any case a dangerous emotion, unbalancing others so that the whole scheme of the self may be upset. So it was with Suzie who, urged on by the perennial impulse to possess, slipped the book under the waistband of her jeans, put on the thick, concealing coat, hurried out of 'Poetry', past 'Paranoia', into the partial freedom of the foyer, out through the revolving metal barriers, behind which the security guard had set up a little sideline of his own, charging ten pence a time as a cloakroom fee, using as a coat stand the many-angled statue 'Holocaust'.

He winked knowingly at Suzie, waving her through. She resisted the desire to show him her handbag, to prove she had nothing to hide. She felt each moment as she negotiated the revolving doors, began the long descent of the stone steps, became aware of the whole orchestra of city, people, movement, meshing around her like a metal cage, she felt that now, and now, and now, upon her guilty shoulder would be laid some heavy hand, into her ear some accusatory word would worm and bloom. And all the while the slim dark book pressed huge and heavy at her abdomen, beat broad and black over her brain like a retributive wing.

She wanted to be caught so it would end. As she neared the bottom of the stone steps she felt at last and with relief, the expected hand. But as she turned towards it she saw that what touched her shoulder, what pressed against her whole frame was not flesh but air, a tidal wave of air which reached her simultaneously with the ugly sound of an explosion. Everything seemed, in that moment, to have stopped. She was the audience of one at the showing of a faulty film. She had never heard a silence so profound as the one which rose out of the descending echoes of noise.

And into that void of inactivity and silence began to crumble the library wall, the roof, the parapet from which the city flag now tilted like a feeble trunk uprooted by a storm. And the wide windows folded in on to themselves like the fabric of an ageing face.

Then the fragments of disintegration began to fall around her, bits of glass and rubble, sections of brick cleaved off as neatly as though destruction were a precision tool. And it was strange, so strange to see the books spew out from the falling building in lazy, somersaulting arcs, some whole, spread open and gliding down like unfamiliar birds; some, disabled, crashing clumsily onto the pavement to lie in little partial heaps, while loose leaves fluttered after them like giant flakes of polluted snow.

It seemed to Suzie this must be a dream, but though she tried to wake from it she could not. And across the square, set into the shadowy protection of a deep doorway she saw a figure which was familiar to her, even through the pandemonium of shouts and screams and breaking glass, through the descending fog of dust which was beginning to obscure everything, she saw Rex.

The sight of him, although it was so brief the space taken by the blink of an eyelid was enough to lose him altogether, convinced her this was no dream. His presence was too real and pernicious. She could feel his physical existence although he was quite distant from her, across the square.

She began instinctively to run in the opposite direction, away from the hurricane of glass and wood and mortar and brick, away from Rex, the force of whose presence seemed to batter at her like a sullen, silent fist. Her face felt wet and warm, and the side of her head. She thought she must have been cut by flying glass. It was possible, too, that she might have been crying, but she could not be sure. She pushed her glasses up onto her nose and ran on as fast as she could across the city, running by memory and instinct, for she could not see, her glasses were misted, perhaps with blood, perhaps with dust.

She was, in any case, seriously disturbed. When she reached the green front door she so far forgot herself as to rush past Rex, who had as usual got there before her, straight in to Larry and blurt out her tale. She must have been seriously disturbed; she had not rushed and blurted for at least five years.

When she had finished she stood before him breathless, dishevelled, on the exact square of hearthrug for which there was no hearth, while he examined her critically over the top of his open newspaper. Finding, even on the most careful inspection, no trace of blood, dust, rubble, gore of any description, he stared at her. There was a long pause during which Suzie heard again, much louder and more terrifying than before, the cacophony of destruction. Then Larry said, 'What is it with you Suzie? What is it?'

Wankel was playing Scrabble with his mother. He thought he would rather have played it with one of Shakespeare's witches. Indeed, nothing could be more witch-like than his mother, stirring her cauldron of letter-tiles, casting her spells over the patterned board. It would not have been so bad if she had lost. But always, somehow, she won. Even if he had been ahead, if all that remained was the placing of a final tile, if he had worked out, logically, that it was impossible for her to win, that there was not the remotest chance of her doing so, still, somehow, she would win.

It was bitter for him, this perpetual defeat at his mother's hands; particularly as it attacked the very basis of his self-pride – his words. For of what use is a poet if he cannot manipulate language, take a word and fondle it warm and malleable, tease it into some desired shape not usually its own, transform it from its habitual conformity to his? Poets are wizards; so Wankel saw himself. But he could not reconcile this image with the consort-witch who sat across the board from him, her knees straddled like ageing fence-posts, her hands blotched with the vitriol of many charms. She worked them still, it seemed to him, in outward innocence, conjuring up from nowhere words he had not known existed, which ate up spaces on the board faster than he could think, which bred double and triple scores off him, even while he was occupied in counting up his own.

It was diabolical. Sometimes when he looked up, the sweat of mental effort beading his forehead (Scrabble was so much harder than poetry, he had found) he half expected to see the fabled horns protruding curved and black out of the sparse white of his mother's combed-back hair.

He had never done so yet. But today she was winning as never before. She was ahead of him from the first word of every game. There was something demonic in the precision with which she selected, sorted, laid out and reckoned up, drawing further and further away from him. Every now and then she took from a paper bag near her elbow, a wrapped toffee, the noise of whose unwrapping nearly drove Wankel to distraction, the noise of whose sucking and savouring caused him, more than once, to leap from the chair and pace about the room, jerkily, like a clockwork toy, while his mother nodded and smiled and sucked and cackled, as benign and apparently untroubled as only victory over a man can make a woman be.

Today he hated her. He had slept badly, uneasy about himself and Suzie. He had woken with the taste of that unease tarnishing his mouth. It had remained with him through a morning spent unfruitfully at his desk. It had followed him across the city to the narrow street in which his mother had her narrow rooms. It had failed to be dislodged by the stink of garbage overdue for collection which hung about the lower hallway. It was with him now, a dull hook on which some element of himself was caught and writhing, while the rest tussled and battled with his mother, and lost.

Today he really hated her. As she leaned forward greedily to place her letters, and he saw how the elastic of her long-legged knickers nipped into the baggy flesh above her knee; as she triumphantly claimed triple word score with the 'z' which he had coveted to complete his own 'zebra'; as she hummed tunelessly and prodded with her tongue the space between denture and jaw, so the hatred rose in him, and he wanted to see her dead.

He wondered whether he was capable of murder; he thought quite possibly that he was. But how could it be done? He was not a practical man; practicality and poetry were unfamiliar bedfellows. The thought of bedfellows drew him back to the conscious contemplation of himself and Suzie. He had felt strange ever since the strange dream provoked by their last meeting; as if some deep disturbance had occurred beneath his outer crust which had irrevocably altered his inner composition. But what precisely had occurred and how, he did not know, it was no more than a sensation of difference, some as yet unidentified rearrangement.

He hooked his bottom lip behind his crooked tooth and tried to improve upon 'and'. He could not, and placed his tiles on the board with a control which quite belied his desire to stamp and swear. His mother grinned at him, inflating the flesh of her cheeks, like an ageing frog squatting the shore of its home pool.

'Y're not doin' too well, Son.' Wankel's mother was enjoying herself; she had not enjoyed herself as much since the last time she had beaten her son at Scrabble. Every line of her told of that enjoyment: the bobbing of her head, a kind of self-congratulatory spasm; the way her eyes crinkled up at the corners in simple glee. Or was her glee so simple? Wankel looked at her carefully to see whether he could discover any hint of malice there; but she seemed all innocence.

At last the final move, over which his mother had deliberated for so long that he imagined her hair whiter and the folds of her face etched deeper by the end of it.

She reached for a toffee and said, as she popped it into her mouth with the satisfaction of a well-won prize, 'Y' didn't do too well, Son.'

Wankel grunted and tried to smile but his lips seemed set. As he put the board away with the toffee-fingered tiles, he again contemplated murder. But it was like a small draught sliding along the very edges of his mind. He was not a man of action; he would never be. He contented himself instead with the visualization of his mother's funeral: a dark limousine, swishing sedately along sodden streets, under a darker sky; no flowers by request; the coffin would certainly be plain; he could not imagine his mother decked out, after her death, in that which she had never been accustomed to while alive. The coffin would certainly be plain. And he, plain, dressed with just the right degree of sobriety (relieved of course by some touch of the poet, some little eccentricity, a turquoise shirt or a pink bow tie), he, alone, leaning back in the corner of the following car. His mother had no friends, or none that he knew of; and he was her only relation. His imagination did not carry him beyond the slow turn through the cemetery gates. He had already depressed himself enough by the contemplation of his solitary journey. Such unaided bearing of bereavement should have caused him to feel heroic; but it was really rather dreary. Even the thought that he might declaim a poem over the falling clods failed to cheer him. For what is the point in a reading, without an audience? His mother would be unlikely to hear him; and as for the attending clergy, they did not count. Cassocks and collecting boxes; there was nothing more to them.

His mother said, through toffee tainted lips, 'Y're lookin' a trifle gloomy, Son.'

Wankel said quickly, as though he had been caught doing something disreputable, 'Oh, no, no; just thinking.'

86

It was perfectly true; but it was not the whole truth. For Wankel's gloom was, to be honest, beginning to be alleviated by the thought that there, behind the cemetery walls, within the exact grey curbstones delineating her grave, his mother would be at last contained, restrained, kept at a suitable distance, visited when – and only when – it was convenient for him, her memory merging with the common past to be extracted and examined with decreasing interest as the years layered themselves upon her, as subtle and concealing as dust.

He was wondering how he could ask her a certain question when she said, pre-empting him, 'Son.'

He said immediately, 'Mother!'

She paused and looked at him. He so seldom called her 'Mother'. He so seldom called her anything at all.

'I thought I ought to tell you,' she said. 'About my Wishes.'

'Wishes?'

'Wishes. After I'm gone.'

'Ah!'

Wankel looked at his fingernails and felt uncomfortable. Death. He with a span of years ahead of him (or so it was necessary for him to believe); she for whom death was a concrete, imminent thing; to confront each other over the very topic which had been the subject of his secret thoughts; he felt discovered. But more than that it seemed to him, as in a flash of revelation which he afterwards wrote in his notebook and marvelled at for months, that death was merely a phenomenon present at the core of everyone, rather like lights or liver, but which expanded as the years went by, more quickly or more slowly according to fate or circumstance, until it swelled through every layer of the self like cancer, and spilled out over the body's boundaries, and all was overtaken by it. It was a fine, but frightening notion. He shuddered slightly, feeling his mother watching him.

'Are y'alright, Son?'

'I'm fine, mother, just fine. It's just that, your – you know; you'll want it plain. Have you – um – reserved a plot?'

His mother began to shake. He wondered at the emotion

sufficiently powerful to move her grinning, toffee-chewing, Scrabble-winning self to tears. But she was not crying. Her shoulders, it is true, were shaking; but to his consternation Wankel saw she was convulsed not with sorrow but with great waves of mirth which formed and broke and formed all through her body until she was a shoreless sea of mirth, dashing to pieces Wankel, his delicacy, his perspicacity.

'A plot?' she said, and wiped her eyes. 'A plot!' she gasped, showing on her exposed tongue the brown mass of a half-ingested toffee. 'You got it all wrong, Son. There'll be no plot for me. I'm goin' t' be cremated!'

Wankel stared at her as though he did not understand. She said carefully, explainingly, as though he were a dull child, 'Cremated. You know. Behind a red curtain. Dropped into the flames while they play "The Lord's My Shepherd".'

Wankel nodded faintly while she lay back in the chair and smiled.

'An' y' know what?'

Wankel shook his head.

'Well. You got no cause to worry about me, Son; no cause at all to worry about your mother. Fer I'm goin' t' have them take my ashes up in a hot air balloon, and scatter them out over the city. A regular little snowstorm, that's what I'm goin' to be. A regular snowstorm!'

As Wankel waited for the No.30, no more than ten yards from the sour odours of his mother's hallway, it began to snow. In every snowflake he saw in miniature his mother's smile; or rather, her demonic leer, for so he now translated it. He thought, she was surely a witch. She had probably been his unloving wife in some former existence, and had entered this in the guise of Mother, to torment him. For I would not have been a good husband, he said to himself in a rare rush of honesty. But I am a poet; and it is impossible to be both a good husband and a good poet. The thought that he might be both a bad husband and a bad poet did not occur to him. He was, after all, Wankel.

Had he been Suzie, he would have pushed his glasses high up

on his nose, demonstrating that he was seriously disturbed. But he looked no more than his habitually tortured self (an image he had cultivated over the years with care – based, perhaps, on an early etching of Shelley). Though to be truthful, waiting for the No.30 with the falling flakes of snow and city grime presenting to him the spectre of his mother's ashes descending in perpetual pollution, Wankel was like an incorrectly made up jigsaw, one piece forced into unwilling juxtaposition with another, the whole tensioned incorrectly, so that the merest nudge buckles and breaks the surface, rendering it not unlike a poxy skin, from whose rising craters may erupt at any moment the suppuration which is gathering beneath.

He was brooding; surveying himself with that solitary inward eye which discovers, under the upturned persona, unspeakable black slimy things with legs. So engrossed was he in his contemplation that he quite forgot to notice and make mental comment on a luscious little piece who came and stood next to him in the queue.

It was not until they had boarded the bus and she was hanging from the handrail like a ripe plum from a summer branch, that he saw her. And even then his interest was minimal. His pulse remained steady. The pupil of his eye – that inverted birth canal from which, spawned in the cold womb of the world, emerges into the mind the wholly formed Idea – did not enlarge. Yet his mind did register that she was a luscious little piece. No more than twenty, with that particular curvature which, from whatever angle it is viewed, gives a satisfying impression of tautness; the kind of tautness which resists the pressure of a passing finger; which causes a tweaked suspender to give off that twang guaranteed to wax the most waning of urges.

He looked at her sideways, leaning back a little so that he could see the fascinating disappearance of the legs under the skirt, the meshing of flesh and fabric which never failed to provoke in him a little anticipatory shudder. This one's legs were particularly good; none of that unbecoming gymnastic muscle; no trace yet of that off-putting stringiness which would surely overtake her by the time she was thirty; (which was just beginning to show in Suzie, though she was remarkably well preserved). No, this one was all softness and curves, just the way a woman should be; and she had on shoes with deliciously high, thin heels – totally impractical for snowy pavements, but totally engrossing in the way they tilted her whole body forwards just the right degree to accentuate those lovely breasts, that bum. . . .

Wankel's mouth began to water. The woman's hip rubbed against his thigh; he wondered whether today might turn into a good day after all. But then the woman smiled at him and said, 'Excuse me', as she reached past him to press the bell. He felt for an instant the startlingly clear imprint of her left breast on his ribs. Then she was moving away from him, down the bus, with a thrust here and a wiggle there which did now send his poet's blood – always so quick to respond to the aesthetic – speeding round the circuitry of tissue and vein.

He watched her go with an inward sigh; but as she stepped down from the bus, she left him, like a parting gift, with a revealing view of thigh and pink lace petticoat which beckoned him irresistibly from between the dark edges of her slit skirt. He thought of Suzie, so trousered, her body zipped into an unalluring case which, he now saw with clarity, was the cause of all his difficulties.

He decided in a flash of brilliance that he would buy her underwear for Christmas. And as the thought formed in his brain, so his brain and eyes focused together on the scene around him, and he saw that the people who were packed into the seats and overflowing into the aisles were nearly all loaded with parcels, boxes, bags and brightly coloured festive wrappings – in short, with all the paraphernalia preceding Christmas.

He thought, gauging the frenetic level of activity in the streets and judging by the haggard faces of the passengers (all, it seemed to him, faded women in headscarves), he thought that Christmas must be happening soon. He decided he would go to the city centre straight away, and choose his Suzie's present there. What might they not accomplish with the aid of a little lace, some lycra?

Wankel spent the rest of the journey in an anticipatory glow. And when he stepped off the bus and slipped on a patch of slush and fell heavily on his hip and took a bruise on it which caused him pain for several minutes, his good humour was not ruffled. He got up and brushed the mud as best he could from his trouser leg and limped, smiling (but not sufficiently to show his crooked tooth) and gallant, into the scented atmosphere of Rookum's.

Wankel had not been into Rookum's for several years; not since the day he had received his last wife's divorce petition. He had been sure it was only the result of his refusal to replace their floor cushions with a three-piece suite; so he had gone to Rookum's to save his marriage and enquire the price of a suite. He had come away reconciled to the divorce; it was so much cheaper.

Now as he pushed through one of the many glass doors which made up the main entrance, and stepped onto the thick pastel carpeting, he was struck once again by the bourgeois vulgarity of it all. He lifted a contemptuous lip and looked down his nose at the middle classes scurrying about their consumer business like so many ants. Soon, he thought, soon. A missionary zeal welled up like saliva under his tongue. Soon the corrupt system would be overthrown, and the People would receive their fair share.

The prospect of it took hold of him so forcefully that he missed his footing on the tricky thickness of the carpet and stumbled sideways. He put out his hand to avoid falling, and found in his grasp a buttock, full and yellow as a rising moon. He looked at it a moment, mystified as to how he came by it, until its owner gave a violent shove which threw him against the plaster nymph guarding the escalator.

When he recovered himself enough to look up he saw the woman (for it had been a female buttock) staring down at him from between mascaraed lashes as brittle and jointed as spiders' legs. Her expression was not pleasant. But Wankel hardly noticed it; for his attention was taken by the sparkle of her earrings (surely diamonds) and the lustrous sheen of the fur she wore draped on her shoulder. Certainly a middle-class matron; undoubtedly an *habitué* of that capitalist fortress, the Conservative Club. He flared a derisory nostril and tried to get up.

Just then the woman opened her mouth. From where Wankel was lying he could see the red glut of her tonsils and beyond, the abyss of her throat. He felt like Jonah confronted by the whale. But before he had time to reach for his notebook and scribble down the idea, a vile screech bounced off his eardrums and caused him to cower back against his nymph for protection.

''Ere!' said the woman. 'Wot the 'ell d'ya think *yore* doin? Shane!' (This to someone behind her, quite concealed by the general bulk and the akimbo arms.) 'Shane! This feller just grabbed 'old of me arse. Wotcha goin' ta do about it?'

Her male protector – he may even have been her husband – stepped around her and looked down at Wankel, who managed to squeeze out, through a constricted throat, 'No, really, I –'

But his words, feeble enough at their inception, were drowned out by the bass guffaw of the man which seemed to originate somewhere in the region of the belly which hung like a filled sack over the low waistband of his trousers.

'Yer arse?' he said, while Wankel watched fascinated as the belly jiggled and swayed. 'You must be jokin', 'Evver. 'E's a bloody poofter!'

Heather closed her mouth with a snap which caused her darkish curls to shake. 'Well! I ask yer! Craig! Dean! Come out of 'ere!'

Two small boys appeared from behind her large legs. One stuck out his tongue at Wankel, while the other began to chant 'Poofter! POOFter!' His mother quickly ended this uncouth behaviour by a well-placed slap on the side of the head. On the child's wail they moved away from Wankel and across the store, ploughing through the people as efficiently, if not as gracefully, as a sailing barque.

Although the whole incident had taken less than a minute, to Wankel, hours seemed to have passed. He got up, nursing his sore hip and his sore pride, and made his way carefully up the escalator to the Lavender Tearoom on the second floor.

He could not resist a quick look in every mirror he passed. What he saw there only partially reassured him, for his hair had grown a little long and ragged at the ends; he had not been exposed recently to much fresh air, poring as he did until all hours over his poetry, and his face had a whitish, unhealthy look to it. And the bones of his face – so fine, so sensitive – did they? Could they?

He stopped in front of a large round mirror in Millinery, to take a better look. His jaw was, perhaps, rather on the small side (it was why he had so much trouble with crooked teeth). And when he put up his hand to smooth back a lock of hair, he saw that his hand was long and white and slender; almost – almost like a woman's hand.

An assistant in a black dress stepped forward with a formidable clearing of the throat and said, 'Can I help you?'

Wankel said quickly, 'Er no, no.' while the woman looked him up and down with a we-see-it-all-here expression on her face.

When Wankel stepped inside the Tearoom, he began at once to feel more comfortable. The room was well-proportioned, harmoniously decorated and quiet. The even hum of voices soothed him, and behind it, the muted strains of Haydn. He sat back in a tapestry upholstered chair and began to feel more as he should, more as a poet should feel. He began, in short, to regain that degree of self-consequence entirely necessary for creativity. The waitress, dressed in one of those nice, old-fashioned little aprons, treated him with respect; and his tea was brought to him in a pot, with a laid tray. The milk was in a jug. Wankel hated little plastic containers whose tops would not come off. The sight of the milk jug gave him a peculiar pleasure; it was nice to have things right. He wondered whether he might not be a little old fashioned at heart. He poured his tea and stirred it and sipped it delicately, and dreamed of Haydn and a more gracious age.

Half an hour spent in this genteel atmosphere, amongst potted palms and softly nodding hat brims, restored Wankel to himself. He did not give a thought to the glorious revolution or the downfall of the bourgeoisie. Such luxuries belong to an equitable frame of mind. Wankel was, just then, entirely concerned with the more basic aspects of existence, self-image, appearance and the like.

And though he was quite restored, he still could not resist, as he left the sanctuary of the Tearoom and made his way to the hurly-burly of Ladies' Lingerie, a quick glance at his reflection in the mirrors he passed. The 'did he?', 'could he possibly?' still lurked in the deeper convolutions of his mind. It was an unfamiliar and pernicious idea. It rippled through Wankel like a stone dropped into a still pool. Even when he was not conscious of the thought it lipped him lightly, took him by the scruff and shook him like an anxious parent.

But twenty minutes of browsing through silk and suspender belts put him entirely to rights. He was not a queer; he could not be. He was a lover of women. If only his women would look as women should. It was not much to ask. He hugged the shallow box of man-made femininity close into his chest as though he wanted to protect some secret there.

'Ah, Suzie!' he murmured as he floated down the escalator. 'Ah, Suzie!' as he pushed out through the swing doors. He was nearly moved to attempt a poem in praise of her. But he contented himself with that other compliment men pay to women, of imagining how she would look in nothing but Rookum's best, ('so suitable for the maturer lady, Sir'), reclining, with a smile of welcome on her wide, wide lips on a background of Bach, and his bed-settee.

Suzie was wondering whether she had made a mistake. The idea at the time had seemed so good. But ideas are wayward things, rather like children, not at all grateful for the miracle of their creation, apt to turn awkward, refuse to conform, bring with them worry or disgrace.

So it was with Wankel's introduction to the Green Street Writers' Group. Suzie could not think why, as the members gathered and she waited nervously for Wankel to arrive, she had

94

ever suggested it. What attraction would 'Poems of Revolution and Revolt' have for their Lady Chairman, Miss Wright? She who favoured gentle verses about Spring; for whom the rhyming couplet reigned supreme; and who moulded her own attempts rigidly on sonnet form. Miss Wright had once referred to Dylan Thomas as a drunken lecher. Suzie always looked upon her afterwards with a strange mixture of contempt and deference. She was, after all, the Lady Chairman, and Suzie had been brought up to respect authority – a notion she had long since logically rejected, but which persisted in a most irritating way in lurking among her actions although it had been banished from her thoughts.

And tonight Miss Wright was at her most formidable. She was already consulting her watch, though Wankel was not yet due. She hemmed, and raised her eyebrows, and drummed her fingers on the table behind which she sat throughout each meeting, like an old-fashioned schoolmistress jealously surveying her class.

Miss Wright was old-fashioned. Suzie noticed it more forcefully than ever now, with the image of Wankel taking up her mind, so avant-garde, so Bohemian. Miss Wright had grey hair pulled into the nape of her neck, there bullied into a small, tight bun. She was tall and large, and her large bosom rested importantly on her uncorseted stomach. She smelled of potpourri and dry rot. You might expect to see at any moment silver fish run out of the folds of her dress. Suzie always stood as far away from her as possible, and if she was forced to accept something from Miss Wright's hand – an agenda, a midmeeting cup of tea – she did so gingerly, employing as little of the surface of her fingers as she could, moving away immediately and wiping her fingers surreptitiously on her thigh, as though there were some contamination there to be removed.

Miss Wright came now and stood so close that Suzie could feel her breath tainting her neck and cheek.

'He's late, this poet of yours!' she said accusingly. 'Everyone's here; we're all waiting.'

Suzie looked round at the five people who were languishing in varying degrees of discomfort on the hard chairs of the Friends' Meeting Hall. It was the only room Miss Wright had been able to hire; writers' groups had got themselves a bad name. Miss Wright could not understand how that was. The vicar, when approached, had said it was all the goings-on. But Miss Wright still could not understand it; there had never been any goings-on at groups where she occupied the chair.

And Miss Wright was in any case pleased with her hire of the Meeting Hall. It had a suitable degree of austerity. Writers, in Miss Wright's view, should neither be frivolous, nor care for the worldly. A spell of conscription would probably improve their work. Failing that, the atmosphere of the hall was, she felt, conducive to that mood of inward circumspection which overtook her whenever she sat down to compose another sonnet in praise of Spring, another story in praise of virtue, whose heroine, we may be sure, always said 'no' in the nick of time.

Suzie took a step backwards and said, with more conviction than she felt, 'Oh! I'm sure he'll be here; any minute, I expect; the buses –'

'Yes, yes!'

Miss Wright had a habit of interrupting in a testy, overbearing way. Suzie had no defence against it; she pushed her glasses up on her nose and looked hopefully towards the door.

Miss Wright said, 'Well. We'd better start,' and banged her gavel on the table with a force quite unnecessary to call to order those whose attention she already had.

She began with apologies, of which there were none, a fact she seemed to consider a personal affront. Then on to publications, under which heading she was sure members would be pleased to know that Mr Morecombe had had a story published in *Latex Life* magazine. Congratulations, Mr Morecombe. A little shower of clapping rippled through the room, like hail on an unsuspecting pond. Miss Wright smiled and bowed as though it was for her. She felt, in a way, as though it was hers. For what was Mr Morecombe but a ruddy blob marring the emptiness of the front row? She was the only person there with soul; the only true creative spirit.

She smiled down condescendingly at Mr Morecombe, who sat so far into his seat he seemed to be moulded there. Suzie wondered whether he was real, or whether he sneaked in before each meeting and placed a likeness of himself there, removing it later when the room was safely empty. But the muscles of his face did seem to twitch as Miss Wright said, 'For our information, Mr Morecombe, what kind of magazine is *Latex Life?*'

Suzie, trying to watch the door and Mr Morecombe at the same time, missed the movement of his lips but caught the words 'general interest'. Miss Wright was asking what sort of story was it? Suzie watched him carefully now but could detect no movement of mouth or jaw; he seemed no more than a well-constructed dummy; but Miss Wright must have heard something for she was saying 'psychological thriller? Ah!' And, always keen to show her superior knowledge, 'Something on the lines of *Hamlet?*'

A small sigh rose from the circle; it could have been relief. *Hamlet*; familiar ground; good old fourth-form Shakespeare – so much more comfortable than this modern stuff, which nobody understood but everyone pretended to. Shakespeare. Ah! They were all talking at once; RSC; GCE; Stratford; Shakespeare. You knew where you were with Shakespeare; that was the thing.

Then Miss Wright uttered an admonitory 'A-hem' and they all fell silent, feeling vaguely chastened although uncertain why. Miss Wright herself was uncertain of why she had stopped them. Only, such unbridled expression of opinion did seem somehow anarchic, unconstitutional; people's behaviour should be regulated, otherwise you never knew where it might end.

The moment Suzie had been dreading now arrived and Miss Wright turned the full power of her gooseberry-tinted eyes on her and said, with that slight hesitation which has difficulty in recollecting a name, 'Er – Mrs Highman! Your poet doesn't seem to be coming.'

Suzie was conscious of them all looking at her. The look was a tangible thing, resting on the surface of the skin and pressing there. She did not know what to say; she felt now that Wankel would not come; it was, in a way, a relief to her; but she felt too, betrayed, with that peculiar shame a young girl feels at the non-appearance of her boy.

'I'll go and look', she said. 'Perhaps –'

But she could not think what the perhaps might be. She went out, bearing the mixed weight of inquisitiveness, irritation, apathy, which made up the atmosphere of the room.

The porchway was stone tiled, cold and damp. The change of air caused her to shiver and draw in a sharp breath; her heels echoed as she crossed the floor. It was very dark, for she had closed the door behind her wanting to shut them off from her completely, to have a time totally alone in which she could collect herself. She could not even see, when she looked over her shoulder, the crack of light showing under the closed door; and the porchway had no windows, no skylight through which she could have seen a streetlamp, or the moon. She did not like such darkness; it was strange, disorienting; she could almost believe her body to be detached from her, as though she were a mind floating in liquid darkness, the world a filled preserving jar set upon a shelf.

She could not find the outer door. She put her hands out, as far as they would reach in all directions, touching nothing. She was afraid to risk a step in case she fell into the abyss of darkness which surrounded like a depthless moat the island where her feet now stood.

From the inner room she heard a high, thin titter; perhaps it was at her expense; the sound of it brought back some measure of reality; she walked forward, and finding the wall with her hands, felt for the metal latch of the door. It was cold and heavy in her hand, she seemed to need all her strength to lift it; the door, too, seemed heavier than she remembered, and swung open very slowly, though she leaned her weight against it.

She hugged her arms tight to her body as she stepped into the street. It was much colder, an unfamiliar cold which reached through her flesh and curled itself around her bones. She looked towards the bottom of the street, then to the top; no one was in sight; there was no traffic, moving or still; not even a dog or a cat nosing the dark doorways. The streetlamps shone on the pavements with an iridescence which mingled with their halos of blue frost giving a queer, blurred look to everything, as though it were seen double, a badly-taken photograph. And it was then that Suzie saw the whole street in ruins; roofless houses, walls collapsed on to themselves, the surface of the road cratered and torn; it was so quiet, so still, as if the movement of a finger might bring down the structures that remained; as though the smallest breath expelled, regret, a sigh, would fold in what was left, reducing all to its original composition: silt, sand, sea.

It was in some strange way familiar to her, as if this knowledge had been born in her, a cell split at her own conception. She could do nothing but acquiesce; although it weighed on her so heavily she was surprised to find she could still stand, could still lift her head.

She heard her name called from the inner room in Miss Wright's imperative voice, and stepped quickly back into the porch. Miss Wright said, 'Well?'

She had left the inner door open behind her and stood now framed against the light – insubstantial, like a silhouette cut out and pasted to a board.

Suzie shook her head and spread out her hands as if to show that she had not made Wankel captive, hidden him up her sleeve. She wanted to tell Miss Wright about the street outside, that everything was over, that nothing mattered now, but she could not think how to phrase it. She knew that Miss Wright would take the ending of the Green Street Group very badly. Suzie felt sorry for her and wondered if there was some way the Group could survive. She wondered how anyone would survive; it was a disturbing thought; she pushed her glasses high up on her nose and wished she had accepted the Book Club's offer of a manual on self-sufficiency. She was not a gardener; she doubted whether she could light a fire. She followed Miss Wright into the inner room feeling rather down.

Miss Wright banged her gavel, causing the air in the room to jump, causing a woman in the back row to wake up and turn down her hearing aid. Miss Wright said, 'Mrs Highman's poet

99

seems to have let us down. I suggest we each read something of our own.'

There was a general rustling and throat clearing such as usually precedes an exposure of the self to the public. Miss Wright folded her large hands across her stomach and, looking as indulgent as her well-trained facial muscles would allow, said, 'Well, now; who's going to kick orf?' There was a little reticent silence, broken by Miss Wright saying, 'Come along now; don't be shy; what about you, Miss Whitehart?'

'Oh, me? I couldn't! No, no! Well – if you really think – I do happen to have a poem with me, a little something I composed on the way, something I was going to ask Mr – er – Wankel's opinion of.'

'Wonderful; wonderful; let's hear it,' said a voice with exaggerated heartiness which nearly, but not quite, concealed its chagrin at not being asked to read first. Suzie thought it was Mr Morecombe's voice, but could not be sure.

Miss Whitehart simpered, stood up, and placed one hand on her bosom, made meagre by a lifetime of unfulfilled yearnings.

'This poem,' she said in a quivering voice, 'is called "Requiem for a Dog"; it is dedicated to the memory of a dear departed.'

Miss Wright murmured, 'Touching; touching.'

The Mr Morecombe voice said, 'You bet.'

Suzie said nothing at all. She was grateful that the moment of her telling them the end had come, had been delayed. And she was, too, fascinated by Mr Morecombe's mouth, its lack of movement; she decided she would ask him, very tactfully of course and after everyone had gone, how he did it. Perhaps it would help her in controlling her own.

Miss Whitehart recited:

> 'I had a dog,
> his name was Fred;
> He lay upon my virgin bed –'

'Rats!' The word cut in rudely from the shadows of the side of the hall.

'Oh, no!'

'Rats, I tell you! Eating the heart out! Gnawing!'

'No!' Miss Whitehart had a horror of rats.

'Where?'

'What, a plague?' The woman in the back row leaned forward anxiously; the commotion had penetrated even the turned-down mechanism of her hearing aid.

'Do something!'

'Rats, eating, gnawing, none of you care, none of you give a damn! That's your trouble, all of you! Rats –'

Miss Wright lunged for the gavel and rapped it sharply on the desk.

'Thank you, Miss Whitehart. And thank you Miss Nutting – no,' (holding up an imperious hand) 'time, I'm afraid, has caught up with us. I hereby declare this meeting closed.' BANG!

Miss Nutting subsided back into the dark corner where she had been hiding and muttered under her breath curses or incantations, Suzie could not be sure. She had been taken by surprise, not having noticed Miss Nutting in the shadows; she blended in them so well, with her dark clothes, her dark hair. Only her face contrasted, so pale it seemed as though the blood had been sucked out of it. Suzie supposed Miss Nutting was mad; people said she was, with her weird wild eyes and her odd behaviour. And she wore men's wellingtons, more than a size too big, and carried – no one knew what – in a spotted cloth slung over her shoulder. She had taken Suzie aside once and told her the cloth contained the secret of existence. She was certainly mad; and yet when Suzie looked at her it was with a kind of longing; for Miss Nutting's mind seemed to transcend the boundaries of custom and convention, to exist in its own unique environment, unhampered by expectation, untainted by regret.

They were getting up and putting their things together. The woman in the back row had turned up her hearing aid. Miss Wright was adjusting her bosom, or perhaps it was her belly; there was no distinct difference marking the separation of the two. Suzie thought, now I must tell them; now. But she could not, and lingered over the teacups in the little tiled scullery, hoping she would be the last to leave.

And it did seem to her, here in the comparative warmth, the light, the company of people who were familiar to her, that her vision of the ruined street had been a dream; the very clarity of her memory made it seem unlifelike. For the memory of reality is often patchy, blurred and indistinct, as though it were necessary for its true character to be stroked out, so that, receiving an impression only, we may translate with maniacal optimism a plight into a circumstance.

And when she had heard them leave one by one and Miss Wright had called to her to remember to lock up, for you never knew who was about, and she had heard Miss Nutting's mutterings rising and falling and growing fainter as she passed the scullery door and went down to the far end of the room, she came out. Mr Morecombe had gone too. Suzie was disappointed; she had so wanted to ask him about his mouth. But perhaps, she thought, pushing her glasses up on her nose, it was better to be on her own; preparing to face the street again she desired no distraction. Perhaps everything was well, for no one had come back; but perhaps, perhaps.

She squared her rather thin shoulders and marched like a new recruit in the army of the world down the central aisle, out through the porchway and into the street, leaving the door this time wide open behind her, so that the light from the inner room spilled out over the drab pavement like yellow paint.

No one was in sight. Suzie looked down to the bottom of the street, then towards the top. Nothing was moving; the street stood whole under a bright moon, so bright that the streetlamps were no more than pale daubs of wash; and the light from the inner room feeble as a struck match.

So it had been a dream. And yet this wholeness seemed no less dreamlike; it was the product of a paintbox, primary and unembellished, drawn out of a child's imagination which has not yet learned the subtleties of translated sight. It was like the glossy picture on the outside of a jigsaw box, which tries faithfully to depict the sum of the pieces that are within, yet which fails in its very wholeness. It seemed to Suzie that behind this bright façade still lay – like rot eating a fruit core where the worm has been – ruin. It was more fearful than the vision of ruin itself. And the silence which surrounded it and her, which lay like a skin of ice casing a turgid pool, was profound. It pressed into her eardrums like a weight of water threatening a diver who has gone too deep. She could not tolerate it, she put her two hands up to her ears and turned back into the porchway, into the inner room which now seemed shadowy, ill-lit, like an unfrequented church.

She collected her things together quickly, not knowing quite what she was doing, but wanting to do something. As she walked down to the front of the hall to pick up her coat she saw, moulded into one of the seats on the very front row, a puppet.

'Well,' said Wankel.

'Well,' said Suzie.

Wankel fiddled with his belt buckle and avoided looking at her. Suzie shuffled from one foot to the other and curved her shoulders in protectively around her rib-cage. She was waiting for his excuse. She thought he would not look at her because he was ashamed. She had noticed an unusual hesitation in him on the telephone, had attributed that too to shame. It made her feel better, almost cheerful; she had not felt cheerful for a long time. Life was so complicated, so unmanageable. She had taken to wearing its difficulties like a sombre cloak which her efforts alone could not throw off. Wankel's excuse would be a help to her; she felt it instinctively. But more than a help; it had come to be in her mind a necessity, something Wankel owed to her, something due from one person to another. For his absence from the Green Street Writers' Group had caused her shame, had made her – which she disliked above all else to be – vulnerable to censure, comment, inquisitive opinion. Wankel's excuse had come to be symbolic, a weighting of the scales between them, which needed to be redressed.

So she came now to his rooms, drab in the flat light of winter afternoon, in a state of expectation. She had not slept well; her night-thoughts, like little pinpricks, punctuating the long hours between sleep and sleep, had been wholly concerned with the possibilities of the excuse. Wankel's death she had had to discount, having talked to him earlier on the telephone. But she discounted it with a certain regret; it would have been the best of all reasons to acquit her in the eyes of the Green Street Group. So next she had dwelt on possible injury, passing a more serene hour than she was used to in the contemplation of two broken legs, a coronary (massive), facial lacerations so terrible that Wankel could not be seen – would never be seen in public again. But these too she had eventually discounted, thinking it likely he would have mentioned them to her, at least when they arranged to meet. Surely he would have said something. Although he was undoubtedly cast in heroic mould he must, she felt, have mentioned something like: 'By the way, you'll have to let yourself in; my wheelchair won't climb the step.' Or perhaps, 'Can you bring a face-mask? My wounds need sterile air.' Or even, 'Mind the electrodes in the hall.'

But he had said nothing, so she was forced back to the contemplation of more dismal ailments like diarrhoea and dementia. Had Wankel gone temporarily insane, and been removed, like laundry, in a plain van? It was, after all, an occupational hazard. Poets were renowned for their peculiarity, were taken away every day. And she had seen about the corners of Wankel's half-closed eyes a certain wildness; though he had seemed as sane as usual on the telephone.

Perhaps, she had concluded with a sigh, the most likely thing was diarrhoea. For men, particularly men such as Wankel, were so very concerned with their insides. Rectal Regularity; Larry had pinned a little plaque bearing these words on the back of the lavatory door the day they returned from their honeymoon. It was probably still there, yellowing and faded, much in the same way as their marriage.

So now she scanned Wankel eagerly, as she stood not quite near enough to the fire, for some sign of interior discomfort. But he moved casually enough about the room, showing no inclination to clutch at his stomach or to pinch his buttocks defensively together. Eventually she cleared her throat and said, 'Er; how are you?'

He looked at her in a kind of absent surprise, as though he had forgotten she was there. Then said, rubbing the back of his neck reflectively, 'Oh; fairly well.'

Suzie thought, 'Broken neck? Fractured collarbone?'

But there was no sign of strapping, and a collar support would surely show.

If Suzie could have seen into Wankel's mind just then – what? It is tempting to say that this or that would have happened differently; but it is also difficult, for we are such rigid creatures, following our mind's determined course, refusing to be deflected from some pre-set aim, refusing to recognize the true perspective; so that our whole life can be composed of insignificancies, which circle us at an increasing rate like water surging to whirlpool; against whose vortex though we struggle, we do not win.

If Suzie could have seen into Wankel's mind, lifted aside a lock of greying hair, drilled through sinew, bone and flesh, drawn out a single cell and held it to the light, seen there the truth, or its approximation – would she have stayed, left, wept, railed? Perhaps none of these things, perhaps several.

For Wankel's hesitation and his unwillingness to look at Suzie were the result not of shame, but of inwardness, that kind of inwardness based wholly upon self-interest. His desire for Suzie was now an abstraction, his proposed possession of her a necessary symbolic act. She was no more than the field on which Wankel battled with himself. For he had to have her; was determined, set, irrevocably committed in his mind to her possession.

And he had so hoped she would wear a skirt. It would have made things easier; he had devoted the whole of the previous evening to the thought of her stockinged thighs, secret under the material of her skirt. He had taken out the box of lingerie, reverently unwrapped its tissued folds, breathed in the distinct and heady aroma peculiar to new nylon; not given one thought to the atrocious cost of inches of lace nothing, a hook, a strap. He had so hoped she would wear a skirt; the prospect of it had thickened up his throat for hours, so that when he spoke to her on the telephone it was with difficulty that the words squeezed out. And now, confronted by her trousered legs, the feeling of disappointment was intense. He wished he could replay the whole scene, send her off to dress as a woman should, bring her back oozing feminine allure, sufficient to excite even the most jaded sense.

For he was beginning to think his senses might be jaded. It was a thought he scarcely dared admit, even to himself; and he only half admitted it, putting it down to vitamin deficiency. He had bought a bottle of iron tablets, taken three, and hopefully flexed his biceps in the shower. But there was no improvement. He decided on drastic measures.

He rippled his vocal cords and said, 'Suzie!'

She hopped as a bird will at the swift pass of a cat's claw.

'I have a confession to make.'

She smiled encouragingly, letting her hands hang open at her sides, a sign, so she had read, of non-aggression. She did so want not to be aggressive. She even forbore to push her glasses high up on her nose, though she would have liked to, in case it could be construed as some kind of threat. She waited, sprung tight despite her apparent relaxation, for the release his excuse would bring.

He came over to her and placed his two hands one on each shoulder and stared at the crown of her head where the hair, he noticed with his poet's eye, grew rather sparse, and the dead looking skin of the scalp could be seen.

'I desire you!'

The air escaped from her lungs in a gusty 'Oh!', the kind of 'Oh!' which reeks of disappointment and dashed hopes. He recognized its down-turned end, and opening his eyes for the first time very wide, stared at her and added, as if for emphasis, 'Madly!'

She said 'Oh!' again, but this time it was a little, sad sound. Wankel could not understand it; declarations did not usually provoke his women like this. He said, rather peevishly, 'It hasn't happened for a long time, you know; not for ages; I was beginning to think – Suzie!'

A shudder had racked her narrow frame, so violently that Wankel felt its vibration rattling the bone of his arm. Perhaps she was crying; he could not see, for her face was turned away from him. He could only see an ear sticking through her hair, an ear which was whitish and flaking slightly around the rim, as though it had been nipped by frost.

Then she did look at him and he saw that she was not crying, although her eyes seemed very large, unusually bright.

'Where were you?'

The surface tones seemed to have been scraped off her voice, leaving it flat and hoarse. Wankel stared at her.

'Where were you?'

Her words were hot with the hiss of escaping breath. Wankel wondered whether she was about to have a fit. Perhaps it was pre-menstrual tension; he had heard that pre-menstrual tension did strange things to women, made them capable of murder, allowed them to be acquitted. He believed it all, and more. For menstruation was the moon-made ritual central to a woman's essential strangeness. Perhaps that was why post-menopausal women were as interesting as shed chrysalides; both gave him the creeps.

He hoped Suzie was not going to be violent; he was not a brave man, he was not – physical. And she was obviously having some kind of turn. He wondered whether she was prone to them; he really knew so little of her, hardly knew her at all; was, really, quite a stranger to her, she to him. You had to be very careful nowadays; he was beginning to see the truth of that.

To gain time, and to avert at least for now the possible attack, he said, 'Where was I?'

'Where WERE you?'

Her voice rose to something near a shriek. Wankel thought, 'Where was I? When? What?' but dared not ask in case the question might sever the last shreds of her constraint, provoke her to violence. She looked as though she would like to hit him. There was a queer green tinge radiating outwards from the pupils of her eyes. Wankel suddenly remembered a wildlife programme about leopards; he shuddered, and hoped she would not choose as a missile his favourite ornament, a statue of Leda being ravished by the Swan.

The green around the irises was deepening. 'TUESday! GREEN Street! You didn't COME! You made me look a FOOL!'

'Me? Come? On Tuesday? Well, one can't always. . . . Ah!'

Wankel stepped away from her, partly for dramatic effect but mainly to avoid the blow which he felt increasingly sure was about to be aimed at him, and clapped his hand against his forehead with a satisfactory smacking sound.

'Tuesday!'

'Tuesday.'

'Green Street!'

'Yes! Yes! Green Street!'

'I forgot.'

'You forgot?'

'Er, yes, that is –'

The eyes were huge now, green and wild and forbidding. If Wankel had needed proof that women were mysterious, dangerous, unpredictable things he had it now. He thought with a speed lent to him by the instinct for self-preservation.

'Yes; forgot. But – but everything, not just Green Street. You see, I had one of my turns.'

'Turns?'

'Yes, turns. Loss of memory. Amnesia.'

Wankel warmed to his theme; he could see the green light going from Suzie's eyes like a receding tide. 'It's something I suffer from; I have for years, or rather' (he amended that hastily; it made him sound so old) 'for the past year or two.' He looked at Suzie from under reticently lowered lids. 'I didn't like to tell you before; I thought it might, well, put you off.' He blinked rapidly, quite moved by his own eloquence, then, unable to read the silence following his words, looked up.

Suzie was smiling at him, a concerned, forgiving, almost maternal smile. The kind of smile maiden ladies of uncertain age reserve for their dogs, fond, foolish. Amnesia! The word had worked on Suzie like a charm; it was the perfect excuse; it would be certain to acquit her down at Green Street; it was so – poet-like; so delightfully eccentric. 'Amnesia!' she repeated it out loud, with a certain reverence, rolling it around her lips and tongue as though it were a favourite titbit, saved at the side of the plate for a last bite.

And had she not read all about it in her *Home Doctor*? Spent half one afternoon devouring its terms, its tell-tale symptoms? Amnesia had a certain stature; it commanded respect; it was the sort of ailment (said her book) peculiar to retired professors and out-of-work philosophers. It had – what was that neat little word everyone was using – kudos. There were times when Suzie wished she had taken Latin at school instead of cookery.

So she looked on Wankel now with favour, especially as he was murmuring into her neck, her ear, her hair, how sorry he was, how terribly sorry.

Suzie did not quite know how they had come together, so close; it must have happened while her attention was elsewhere, focused perhaps on the vision of her triumphant return to Green Street. But here they were, close, rib against rib, breath mingling ever so slightly with breath. It was not unpleasant; quite nice, in a mild kind of way. And as Wankel drew her towards the settee (he disliked the crudity of the outright suggestion, bed, and besides, it was so much warmer here, he having left the fire on two bars since breakfast time, despite the expense), as he drew her down to the settee and began to peel off, artistically, layer after layer of her clothes, she continued to think it quite pleasant. But her mind was not wholly on it; little pictures kept appearing in her brain, variations of the scene at Green Street, what she would say, what they would say, how Miss Wright would look, disappointed, impressed.

As she lay on the settee naked and feeling rather cold despite the two bars of the fire and noticed Wankel emerging nimbly from his white cotton underpants, bending forward to see them safely over his bare toes, thrusting his buttocks (which were surprisingly large) towards the net draped window, she thought, in repetition, as though it were some clockwork chant implanted in her head, Rectal Regularity, again and again,

Rectal Regularity. She pinched herself, hard, on the back of the thigh. The words slowed in her head like the running down of an old gramophone and stopped. Wankel lowered himself on to the settee beside her. It reminded her of a picture she had once seen of a sperm-whale being winched aboard a factory ship.

He said, 'Bit of a squeeze, eh?'

She put out her hand tentatively and said, 'Um; they're awfully big.'

Wankel followed the direction of her look and peered inquisitively over the rise of his belly.

'Oh; er; I meant the settee, actually. But do feel free.'

'Sorry.'

Suzie fluttered her hand back disconcerted, and laid it on her leg. There seemed nowhere else to put it; she felt suddenly hot, ashamed. She wished Wankel had not removed her glasses; she would have liked to push them high up on the bridge of her nose. She wished Wankel would do something. Men ought to do things; she did not know what to do. Her hand rested heavily on her thigh; she felt Wankel's hip-bone pressing uncomfortably into her stomach, and his skin, rather sticky and hot.

Wankel did nothing because there was nothing he could do; or nothing much. What was the point in starting something you could not finish? The trouble was, flesh was so flesh-like. Seeing Suzie exposed to him on the settee he was reminded of a nest of young mice he had found once in a harvest field, motherless and moving a little, white and pliant under his probing finger, strangely repulsive.

If only she had had on a skirt; or even some of those little lace panties which curved up over the buttock to a single strip of silk. He did not ask much; surely femininity was a right all men could expect.

Suddenly deciding he said, 'I've got something for you.'

She looked at him.

'I haven't had time to wrap it.'

She looked down, doubtfully; she did need glasses, even so. . . .

'Oh, no, no; I mean, a present.'

He reached across her and drew out from under the settee the box of lingerie.

'For me?'

'For you.'

She pushed herself up on one elbow and smiled at him gratefully. He really was quite sweet; so thoughtful of him, a gift, saved till now. She looked at the plain box wonderingly. Books? It did not feel heavy enough, although she had mentioned, quite innocently, that she was collecting a set of leather-look Dickens. Records perhaps? Bach, Vivaldi; she hoped it was not Bach; she had been planning to give Wankel Bach for Christmas; he was so fond of Bach. But it was the wrong shape for records; what, then? What did men give women? It was so long since a man had given her anything. Years ago, when she was a student, the vulgar joke had been, chocolates, flowers and the clap. She wondered whether Wankel had ever had the clap; was it possible to tell by looking at someone?

'Aren't you going to open it?'

'Oh. Yes.'

She fumbled, awkward and one-handed, with the folded cardboard. He helped her, eager now and feeling an interest stirring. When the lid had been lifted, the tissue paper drawn back, and the glorious, frothy, feminine contents revealed, there was silence. Suzie did not know what to say. She thought of her own plain cotton knickers lying somewhere on the floor in a little self-effacing heap (gusset, she hoped, turned modestly inwards).

She did not feel equal to all this gaud. She disliked it, no, more than that, hated it. Lace next to her skin brought her out in spots; and nylon was so sticky, slimy at the folds of your flesh.

Wankel touched the material with his fingers and said, 'Aren't they beautiful? Won't you try them on?'

Suzie said, 'Do you think they'll fit?'

'Oh, I should think so; they're quite flexible,' (picking up a black net suspender belt and drawing it out wide between his hands). 'See?'

'Well. If you think so.'

'Oh, I do, I do.'

But how to put them on? She did not want to stand up, to be entirely vulnerable to the unflattering afternoon light. She wished, regretfully, for the convenience of a Victorian screen behind which she could retire modestly and emerge transformed. But there was no screen, nothing to help her, so she struggled prone and uncomfortable under Wankel's intent stare into black silk stockings, suspender belt, panties, while he made appreciative noises such as she herself sometimes made over a rare rump steak.

She said, as he offered her another strip of nylon, 'Oh, no thank you. I don't wear a bra. Women's Lib, you know.'

The words 'Women's Lib' came out on a self-conscious little titter; she felt somehow that Wankel would be sure to despise Women's Lib, although they had not discussed it. And she did so want Wankel not to despise her. He said nothing, merely looking disappointed and hanging the bra by one strap over his wrist, and swinging it backwards and forwards like a twin-gonged pendulum.

'Well; if you'd rather not. But it's not much of a bra, honestly. See – it hasn't even got any, er, centre bits. Your – that is, you wouldn't feel, um, constricted or anything.'

Then, in the manner which when employed by small boys Suzie strongly disapproved of, but which now, employed by this larger boy, she suddenly found excusable, Wankel said, 'Couldn't you? Just for a little while? It would be so –'

Suzie's resolution crumbled. She was powerless before his entreaty, his winning smile and the wistful lift of a greying brow. He made her feel so unreasonable in denying him. After all, what was a strip of nylon one way or the other. So she acquiesced, and slipped the bra over her arms with as much grace as if she were a horse put to harness, while a sour mixture of contempt and humiliation washed the back of her throat like bile.

Wankel said, 'You look wonderful.'

Suzie said, 'Thank you,' and put her hand up to her nose,

forgetting there were no glasses there to be adjusted. She wondered what would happen next; she supposed something would happen; she looked at Wankel expectantly.

Something had happened. Wankel was delighted, jubilant, almost as ecstatic as when his first poem had appeared, in *Radox* – really *Radix* but the subject of an unfortunate printer's error. He opened his arms and legs as widely as the settee would allow, wishing he had opted for the bed, closed his eyes, covered his crooked tooth and murmured, 'Ah, Suzie! Take me! Use me!'

'I beg your pardon?'

He opened one eye, then the other. 'Take me. Use me.'

Suzie looked blank. Wankel lifted his head an inch and said incredulously, 'Take me, use me. You know; like Dante said to the Muse.'

'Oh. I see.'

Wankel levered himself up on one elbow and looked at her. He tried to tell himself she was a remarkable woman for thirty-three but could not. She really was hopelessly – well, hopeless. Desire for her drained from him; he could feel it seeping through his flesh like the lowering of a water table.

Suzie saw, and wondered whether it could be her fault. She did not think so; she had heard it happened to men of Wankel's age. He managed a weak smile and said, 'The, um, excitement seems to have been too much for me.'

Suzie nodded.

'Well.'

'Well.'

They both got up, stiff-legged with their backs to one another, and began to dress. Wankel was ready first and put on some Bach. He felt better at once. There was nothing like a little Bach; he was so fond of Bach.

Suzie took longer. She felt in some way she did not understand, that she had failed, whether him or herself she was not sure. But what else could she have done? The lace was already making her itch, and the folds of her flesh felt slimy where the nylon was. She sipped the coffee that Wankel made without tasting it, without, really, being aware of what she did. Life was so difficult, so complicated. It settled on her with such a weight as she hurried home through the short and unfriendly twilight, that not even the prospect of her triumphant return to Green Street could cheer her.

Herbie Greengage was sitting in Suzie's through-lounge feeling blue. He said, first to himself then to the empty room (for Suzie was making coffee in the kitchen): 'I'm feeling blue.' And again, with a sigh, 'I *am* feeling blue.'

He had come on what he called the off-chance, between clients you know, just time for a quick cup. The truth was, he had experienced during the backstreet drive between the Farahdil Bankrupt Cloth warehouse and the Shamil Aziz flood damaged carpet store (half price) an overwhelming feeling of gloom.

For trade was going to the dogs; worse, to the wogs. You only had to take a look around you to see who the hustling, bustling entrepreneurs were these days. Sham-Alla Brothers Used Cars; Too-Hyya Superstores; it was all the same; there was no room for a decent Jewish middleman anymore. And what were all his cousins and his uncles doing, his own brothers? He squeezed a disgusted little sound out through his teeth. Doctors, dentists, opticians; fools, every one. The only one with any sense was his second cousin by marriage, Joseph, who was running his own ice-cream van. That was the one who would get on. 'My life,' he said; and again, out loud, 'Fools, every one.' Couldn't they see that all you needed was energy, determination and a certain flexibility as to the truth? And Bingo! There you were. Nice little wife; nice little car; nice little house in its own twenty acres.

He brightened for a moment at the thought of these, his three favourite possessions (though not necessarily in that order); but the gloom descended again almost at once. That was how it used to be; but now, what was it all for? Between them – the wogs and the taxman – there would soon be nothing left. It was a poor future in store for young Benjie, after his days. Funeral directors and death duties; he doubted whether Benjie could expect more than a hundred thousand or two.

Herbie Greengage was not a man given to introspection. But the feeling of gloom, the dark prospect of his future and his son's, had turned his thoughts inwards and at the same time backwards. Driving across the city he had seen, wistfully and fleetingly, an image of the younger Herbie, poorer it is true, but infinitely more carefree, more optimistic; and in the throes of his first, fumbling passion, his affair with Suzie, which had passed through six seasons of indecision before its final ignominious resolution – Herbie's abandonment in favour of Lanky Larry, who according to Suzie was possessed of 'more soul'.

Not that Herbie had regretted his loss once in the intervening seven years. Suzie was so neurotic, as well as being inconveniently flat-chested (oi-veh! those ribs!). But today the image of youth and university had awakened in him something, some undirected longing, and he had decided to Look Suzie Up.

And the passage through the vaginal hallway did seem a little like rebirth. So long as you remembered not to look out of the window you could think you were in another world. Books; Breughal prints; the girl had taste, there was no doubt about it. Such taste made it almost possible to ignore the exterior prospect, looming large in the middle distance, of twin cooling towers and a disused gas holder.

And as she came in now, looking slightly harassed with her hair in the habitual disarray which he remembered from their student days, and her thin shoulder blades braced against each other, awkwardly balancing two mugs in her hands, he felt a sudden rush of desire; for Suzie, for youth, for the old days; for 300 per cent mark-ups and 4 per cent inflation.

As he took his mug he let his hand touch hers lingeringly. Her flesh was cold; it had always been cold, even when she was eighteen, cold and pale and then as now, suddenly, infinitely desirable. He cleared his throat, discovering an unexpected huskiness there and said, 'Your hands are still cold.'

'Still?'

'They always were; don't you remember?'

And as he said it Herbie himself remembered more than cold hands. He remembered her long, thin, cold body pressed against his on numerous unsatisfactory nights; nights when the presence of her flesh had been tainted by the absence of her mind, loose somewhere beyond the cast of his net, its current subtly disturbing, strangely disconcerting. He felt it now, this peculiar absence; she was there yet not there. He fancied for a moment that he was in the company of her ghost. He laughed nervously, giving himself a mental shake for such morbid fancy. He was not usually a fanciful man; he dealt with the realities of life: figures, percentages and the like. He said, 'You're looking real good, Suzie.'

She said, 'Am I?' in a neutral, absent way. She had forgotten just then that Herbie was there, even though he was sitting opposite her. She had so many things on her mind: Wankel; and Wankel; and the chairperson of WAG had been leaving threatening messages about her article. She was now afraid to answer the telephone and had taken, during the day when the lodger and Larry were out, to bolting the front door, in case the WAG executive attempted a forced entry. She had only let Herbie in because she had sneaked a look from an upstairs window and recognized his Rolls.

And she regretted now that she had let him in; for his presence disturbed her; old images, sepia-tinted, flickered at the edges of her thoughts. She pushed her glasses high up on her nose and said, 'Um, how's Miriam?'

Herbie, in the middle of sipping his coffee, gulped and coughed. Miriam. So round; so ripe; so ready. The epitome of young motherhood; he pushed the thought away from him, like a pudding found too sweet at the eating.

'She's fine; just fine.'

'And Benjie?'

'Oh, he's fine too.'

The truth was, he had had to think for a second before remembering how Benjie was. For Benjie, in proportion to the amount he had begun to squall, had begun to pall. The sight of him sucking energetically at Miriam's large nipples had also lost its attraction; particularly at midnight when he would have preferred they were offered to him.

He put down his mug and looked at Suzie earnestly. She smiled back at him in a preoccupied, friendly way. She was wondering whether she had heard someone trying the front door latch; perhaps it was the WAG executive. She would have liked to hide in the kitchen but was afraid Herbie would think her odd. He said, 'Suzie –'

Just then there was a rattling from the direction of the hall like a letterbox being opened and closed, or a handle shaken. Suzie jumped up and ran into the kitchen. Herbie was mildly surprised. But Suzie had always been impulsive; her going to bed with him all those years ago had been on the strength of an impulse. She hadn't changed much; but that was one of the strange things about women, they didn't seem to change. Herbie supposed it was to do with their reproductive function. If you were going to keep the species going, it stood to reason you wouldn't have much time to mess about with change and development. He sighed at the prospect of thirty years of unchanging Miriam. His little Miri; in a mink at thirty; in corsets at forty; unimaginable at fifty. What did become of luscious, little-girl women? He stifled a shudder and wondered where Suzie had got to. Had she been taken short, maybe? She had been a great one at university for getting taken short. He showed his teeth at the memory of how she always had to sit right by the exit in the lecture theatre, so she could make a quick dash if the need arose. Oh, boy! Those were the days!

He slapped his thigh with more gusto than for a long time, and went in search of Suzie. He found her in the kitchen, her narrow frame pressed into the small space beside the refrigerator. He said, 'Hey! What's this?'

For she was looking rather pale and her eyes were very big. His voice seemed suddenly unnaturally loud so that it was almost reasonable for Suzie to screw her face up and 'sssh' him. He went and stood very close to her and whispered into her ear, 'What is it?'

She said, 'Someone at the door.'

Herbie said, 'So?'

Suzie said, 'It might be someone I don't want to speak to.'

Herbie said, 'But it might be someone you do want to speak to.'

Suzie looked at him. He was just the same! No soul! They were planets apart.

Something of her thoughts showed in her face; Herbie recognized the look but before he could quite recall which of Suzie's looks it was, he became aware of something stronger and more pressing. The closeness of her thin body, the smell of her hair and skin, quite unmistakable even after such a lapse of years, and rising strongly to his nostrils as he bent to catch her whispered words – even the look itself, in its familiarity – all combined, so that he found himself thinking, without meaning to, of her actual possession, how it might be accomplished, then, there, in the kitchen of her own home, with the dregs of the coffee cooling in the other room, and the real prospect of Larry's imminent return. The thought of Larry steadied him slightly so that he merely grasped her arm and said, 'Suzie! You and I! We could do great things together!'

Suzie, paying no attention, tried to 'sssh' him, for she thought she could still detect some movement outside the front door. But the pursing of her lips in readiness gave Herbie ideas, or rather, gave direction to the ideas he already had; and Suzie found herself, in the words of many lady writers of romance, being thoroughly kissed.

If this were one of those romances, no doubt Suzie would fight tigerishly to preserve her virtue, or else, feeling dizzy with passion, sink out of sight behind the turned page and succumb. But Suzie did neither of these things. In fact, she hardly noticed what was happening, so intent was she on listening for potential entry via the front door. And besides, Herbie was so familiar. By the time their affair came to an end she had viewed his presence rather as one might view the presence of a television set – necessary to vary the boredom of a winter evening. So it was not until she felt the cold pressure of the vinyl floor tiles against a newly-bared area of her spine, and heard Herbie muttering something which sounded like 'real woman; real mind', that she realized his intent.

And though it may seem strange, she neither struggled nor responded. Herbie's assault (for assault it was, despite his murmuring as many persuasive endearments as he could remember) was merely one event among many. The lodger, the library, Wankel, Green Street, WAG – they were all like film strips, edited imperfectly, passing before her in a mêlée of contradiction and disorder, which she had formerly tried to organize and control, but which she now began to perceive as being beyond her. She heard Herbie say, 'Is it safe?'

She did not understand what he meant. Surely he knew that nothing was safe, that living was an unsafe business, dangerous, unpredictable?

She felt his lips on her neck and the weight of his body beginning to press on her. The floor felt hard under the back of her head and there was a low draught which chilled the flesh of her now bare hips. She thought about her article, how she might fit Herbie into 'Sex and Intellect'. Perhaps she could put him under the heading 'Ethnic Minorities: their peculiarities'. But she had begun to doubt that she could complete the article at all; there seemed so much to say, but when she came to say it, so little.

Herbie's breath was rasping in her ear and she turned her head away to avoid it, noticing as she did so a crust of bread lying near to her, dropped she supposed from the morning's breakfast scraps. Its presence annoyed her. She disliked dirt. It would be sure to bring in mice, and Larry would set traps. She hated to trap mice. As a small child she had watched her father handling calculated bits of cheese, softening them with the flame of a lighted match, impaling them on the spiked prong, setting the spring, carefully keeping out his fingers in case they should be bruised by that which would snap the mouse's spine in two.

She felt in some way that this epitomized men in relation to women. She had intended to use it in her article but had been unable to work it through. She found difficulty in thinking about

119

it in a clear way, for whenever she tried her head filled up with the sound of the mouse's scream, the one mouse who lay all night in the attic behind her bed, separated from it by only a thin partition, agonized by the imperfect working of the trap, until her father took it in the morning still screaming into the darkness of an old outhouse, and killed it there, by what means she had never found out.

She moved uneasily, wondering what Herbie was doing. He seemed to be grunting a lot and weighed on her rather heavily. But he was distanced from her by the shadow of memory, which fell large across her brain, so large that she imagined for a moment it was real and falling across her and Herbie on the kitchen floor. She blinked and shook her head slightly to rid herself of it. But it would not go and stationed itself unmovingly over them, so that Suzie at last looked up and saw, pressed close against the window pane, the silhouette of a pair of shoulders and a head.

Her scream rivalled the mouse's *in extremis*. Herbie gasped, 'Hey! Wha' did I do?'

But before he could find out, Suzie had thrown him off her and was struggling to her feet, miraculously adjusting hair, clothes, mind, so that in seconds she was no more than her normal dishevelled self, and talking to the window cleaner through the back door, passing him with a hand which barely shook, two pounds instead of one. When she came back into the kitchen Herbie said, 'Who? What?'

She took her glasses off and put them back on again and said, 'The window cleaner; he climbs over; I let him. Er – do you mind?'

Herbie was still lying on the floor, his back angled now against the wall, his head lolling on one side as though it were too heavy for him. He had not – as the polite phrase is – adjusted his dress; a minor matter which he had forgotten in the terror of the moment, thinking that Larry had come home, thinking he was caught in the act. And relief at the words had driven all thought of propriety out of his mind; in any case, what was a little bare flesh between friends? But now seeing how Suzie looked at him, he began to feel rather foolish, rather exposed, and got to his feet pulling up his trousers at the same time, something he had not tried to do since Miriam's mother had gleefully discovered them together, and demanded that he make an honest woman of her daughter.

He was the victim of a number of conflicting emotions. Disappointment, frustration, a queer sense of *déjà vu*, as if this were merely a repetition of his and Suzie's perennial inability to get it – whatever it was – together. But chiefly he felt relief, not unmixed with surprise that he was relieved. He wondered whether attempted suicides felt similarly. For he had been on the brink of making a mistake, the kind of mistake which can wreck men's lives, turn them to drink, cause bankruptcy. He adjusted his tie and wondered how quickly he could leave.

Suzie, looking at him from across the vast gulf measured by three feet of tile, was wondering the same thing. And she was thinking too, how odd it was that she had forgotten the way his body hair grew thick and wiry, covering chest, shoulders and belly like some strange variety of curly-coated monkey. Then again, how short his legs were, how flat and archless his feet, even in his built-up shoes.

She wished he would go. She wished she could say 'please go'; but she had never learned the art of outright rejection, so she said instead, 'Will you have another coffee?'

And Herbie, to whom saying no presented not the least difficulty, said, 'Er gee, er no, er thanks all the same. I gotta blow.'

Walking the length of the through-lounge allowed him time to feel some compunction. Of course, it was Suzie's fault really. She had led him on; women always led you on. But perhaps he should say something; she looked kinda scrawny, and down. He stopped at the door and said, 'Er, look Suzie –'

He saw that she was looking beyond him, over the top of his head as if she expected something to materialize there. He said, feeling absolved, 'S'long; nice seeing ya.'

And she said, 'Um; yes,' not having heard anything he said,

willing him to go quickly so she could retreat behind the safety of the green front door.

Herbie wrapped the full part of his lips round his teeth and pressed what remained briefly against Suzie's cheek. As soon as he turned from her she stepped back, closed the door and slid the bolt across.

Herbie was unaware of it, waved a casual goodbye to the empty path, drove off. For his mind was already occupied elsewhere. What a crummy street this was, a crummy neighbourhood; almost as bad as where he had lived in his student days. His nostrils twitched and the tiny muscles behind his ears tensed and shivered; if he were a dog, his tail would have begun to wag. For he had scented an idea. Maybe he should buy up a few of these joints, rent them out to wogs and students. You could really pack 'em in, students and wogs; they would never complain. Maybe he'd get cousin Joseph to come in with him and manage the deal. He slapped his thigh. Holy Moses! He'd make a packet.

The Rolls-Royce jumped and swerved, narrowly missing a parked motorcycle. But Herbie's good humour refused to be impaired; he was on his way to Miri, and another million. And in a moment the car swung sedately out of the narrow street where Wankel's Suzie lived, and joined the flow of traffic moving across the city.

Suzie is sleeping. You can tell she is sleeping from the way her arm rests casually across Larry's thigh. If she were awake the smallest contact of her flesh with his would cause an immediate withdrawal, a reflex action seated as deeply in the brain as that which causes the snatching back of a finger from flame.

Larry is not sleeping. Although it is past midnight the light on his side of the bed is on; he is, as usual, reading. His quota of newspapers for the day has not been reached; he has not acquainted himself with every item, all the numerous different accounts of what is going on in the world. He has not sufficiently kept up with things.

And although Suzie's arm across him is an irritant, the part where flesh meets flesh moist and clinging, like a leech which ought to be brushed off before it sucks out something, he has allowed it to remain, afraid perhaps that any attempt to remove it will wake her, or that such movement will involve more bodily contact that there already is.

It is quite quiet, or as quiet as a city can ever be. For a city is no more than a vast and cumbersome machine, the cogs of which sometimes slow a little but never fall still. Existing in a city is inhabiting these corridors of cogs, is learning to step effortlessly in and out of the slow-moving grooves, to dodge the meshing of metal teeth. It is acquiring the art of ignoring the inevitable accident, some fellow dweller caught and crushed. And Larry, as a city dweller must, has learned to close down certain areas of his senses, blunt at will the antennae which in a natural state are constantly receptive to the minutest stimulus. So that now, he is quite unconscious of the muted hum of the machine, so unaware that if you asked him he would say there was no noise at all, all he could hear is silence.

Suzie has never managed to deceive herself so far. Her socialization into the brotherhood of cogs has been imperfect. And when she is asleep as now, her antennae work their best, and she is uneasily aware of all that lies just outside herself: the room, the house, but most of all the city itself, strangely magnified, vibrating in the nucleus of her every cell, pressing outwards from inside, inwards from out, so that the whole structure of cell and self is infiltrated by it, threatened. For if the balance should alter, a sudden stress would be set up, causing the structure to weaken dangerously.

It is this awareness of the city, of Larry and the light and the pages of the newspaper casting at each turn a shadow across her, like the slow wing of some gigantic moth, which sets her dreaming.

In her dream she is standing in an empty street – perhaps it is Green Street, the houses seem like those in Green Street; and suddenly from every doorway, like the accelerated figures of a weather vane, people step out. The whole street is lined with them at intervals so exact they might be sentries; and they turn towards her with the precision of a sentry duty or a guard, the same exactitude of timing. As they approach, slow and wooden, she can see that they are familiar to her. In the background, the Green Street Group; in the middle Herbie, Wankel, Miriam with the inevitable bundle resting in the crook of her arm; and nearest, nearest of all, the WAG executive. As they come closer she can see that they are made of wood, all of them, their features crudely applied with paint. And out of one door – the nearest to her, which she had not noticed was still closed – comes another figure, no wood this, larger than the others with a special, separate presence. They all stop moving except this last, and their jaws open and close like wooden traps. Sounds come out: words, accusations, expectations – why didn't you, when will you, what about, over and over again – and still the one figure coming on, coming on, Rex, growing larger by the instant, more terrifying, watching her, always home before her, Rex, whose silence is itself an accusation, who does not turn as the wooden figures split open like cracked eggs, from each one emerging lithe and full of life Rex replicas, identical, exuding power and vitality, all advancing on her at a run.

As the first one reaches her and grabs her arm she screams, a terrified despairing sound which echoes through the houses of the street, coils round their foundations, takes them and shakes them as though an earthquake had occurred, collapses them to rubble. And from the rubble rises like smoke out of a genie's lamp, a sigh, her name, Suzie, Suzie. . . .

'Suzie! Suzie!'

Slowly Suzie swims up out of the street, loose of the grasping hands, above the tidal shudder of the settling walls, up through the pool of her mind whose surface she breaks reluctantly to find, between her and the bedside light, the face of Larry, like a darkened moon, whose hand is clasped around her wrist as if to fend her off, whose lips, stiff as a wooden trap form the familiar words, 'What is it with you Suzie? What is it?'

*

Wankel was in a mood as near self-doubt as he would ever approach. He avoided going to see his mother, though a visit was due; he felt, in his present fragile state, that such a visit might depress him, and he did not want to be depressed. For depression might subdue the creative urge vital to the timely completion of 'Bolshevik Love Poetry'; for which his up-and-coming agent swore he had an eager publisher, whom he was strangely reluctant to name.

But still, despite not visiting his mother, the self-doubt, or its Wankel equivalent, was rapidly turning into just the depression he wanted to avoid. He was not sure what to do about it. He moped in his room giving great attention to the width of his lapels, wondering whether their style, which was a little out of fashion, was unflatteringly ageing. For women paid such attention to these things. He thought, with a contemptuous curl of the lip, that Suzie probably paid attention to them.

But he had to admit there was more to it than lapels. The basis of his problem was lust. Not that he had anything against lust; far from it; lust was a lovely thing; lust made the world go round, ring-a-ding-ding. If only it would make his world go round. He felt rather like a motor car whose engine works perfectly but whose wheels, for some unaccountable reason, will not turn. It was very frustrating. It had begun to give him headaches and he felt it might soon put him off his food; he hoped a cure could be found before any such drastic effect occurred.

He decided he would go to the doctor. Perhaps the doctor could prescribe a tonic; that was all he needed; he had probably been working too hard; 'Bolshevik Love Poetry' was heavier going than he liked to think.

So two days before Christmas Eve, Wankel set off in his clerical coat and with a striped scarf knotted carelessly about his throat, for the Inner Lazarus Street health centre. At the last moment he had hesitated, thinking perhaps he felt a poem coming on, but it had passed off, so, contenting himself with putting a dyspepsia lozenge under his tongue in case the feeling should return, he went.

The pavements were very crowded which puzzled him until he saw the tinsel stars in the shop windows and heard the tinny sounds of pre-recorded saintliness trickling out of the doorways. The third time he was waylaid by a Salvation Army bonnet menacing him for money he almost turned back; but he struggled heroically on, elbowing his way through a forest of spongy stomachs and hard hip-bones until he half-fell, half-staggered into the antiseptic atmosphere of Community Health.

Wankel was rather dazed. It was all so different from the way doctors' surgeries used to be. A sign on the wall near him said 'Hernias Straight Through'; another said 'IUD – The Facts'. Wankel was surprised at that one; he thought Rhodesia had been settled years ago. He decided he should read more newspapers, for it didn't do to get out of touch. He looked round for a receptionist, but all he could see were dozens of people trying to sit upright in tubular steel low loungers. He supposed this must be the waiting room, and these the patients. When he saw how they all avoided each other's eye, he was sure of it.

Then he noticed next to a potted palm in the centre of the room, two women in white coats sitting behind a sign which said 'May We Help You?' As he looked towards them they smiled identically encouraging smiles and called out in unison, 'May We Help You?'

Wankel sidled over to them, uneasily aware of the numerous eyes watching him, and asked to see a doctor.

'A doctor?' said the one, who looked not unlike a younger version of his mother.

'A doctor?' said her echo.

They looked at each other, then at Wankel, then back at each other. They were no longer smiling. The one leaned forward and said, as though he were a small boy who had misbehaved himself, 'This *is* Community Health, you know. Now, may *we* help you?'

A queer feeling began to tickle the back of Wankel's throat; it might have been desperation. He said, 'But isn't this the surgery? I need to see a doctor. I'm, er, sick.'

The women exchanged the kind of look which acknowledges

126

a difficult customer. The elder of the two whose hair, Wankel noticed, was done rather like the Queen's, said, 'Well; it all depends; what seems to be the trouble?'

Wankel muttered something about 'overtired' and 'hard work', aware of all the ears straining to overhear him. He kept his voice very quiet and his back turned to as many as he could, but he was one against a roomful. And in any case it was no use, for the next moment the younger of the white-coated two said in a routine, efficient, we-see-it-every-day loud hail, 'Brewer's Droop, eh?'

And the elder, not noticing perhaps how Wankel winced and cowered, said: 'Brewer's Droop? Doctor Alright, Room Three. He's our Brewer's Droop man. Wait for the light.'

Wankel slunk away from her dismissive shoulder and huddled himself into an empty chair. He was reaching for the only available magazine, something called *Petticoat*, when a voice said, 'Er; hello.'

The outstretched hand snatched back from the cover of *Petticoat* as though it had detected there something vile. Wankel looked at Suzie and managed the outline of a glum smile and said, 'Um; hello; fancy seeing. . . .'

And Suzie pushed her glasses up on her nose and said, 'Um; yes; small world. . . .'

They exchanged the usual pleasantries, the what-a-surprises, the nothing-serious-I-hopes, then a silence developed because they could think of nothing else to say.

Wankel thought, how like a woman to turn up at just the wrong time. Suzie thought, he doesn't seem very pleased to see me. She put her hand up to her mouth, whose growth was becoming more difficult to contain since Herbie Greengage's visit, and wished it was time for her to go in.

She was not really sure why she was there, what she could say was the trouble. But her *Home Doctor* gave no information on spreading mouth. And then again, she thought if only she was not so tired she might be able to finish her article; it would be so convenient to be able to answer the telephone again. And all the running up and downstairs to bolt and unbolt the front door was giving her over-developed calf muscles. So she had decided in a rare fit of resolution that something must be done.

And there was, it must be admitted, another reason for her visit. Larry, unusually loquacious, had said to her over that very morning's cooling toast (the papers, for that moment only, laid aside), 'You should see a doctor, Suzie. You're nuts.'

These words, endearments, call them what you will, had a profound effect on Suzie; or, to be more precise, Larry's laying aside of the newspapers to utter them did. And what was more she could not deny that she had recently been experiencing queer stretching feelings somewhere inside her skull; rather like over-taut elastic which cannot decide whether to snap or become permanently flaccid. She could feel the beginnings of the sensation now, and tried to relax but could not with Wankel's indifferent knee only an inch from hers.

She looked again at the row of lights but Room Four, where she was supposed to go, remained unlit. And then, becoming aware of a kind of rustle passing through the room, a subtle straightening of male backs, and the sigh of trousered thighs rubbing together, Suzie looked towards the door.

Miriam saw Suzie straight away and waved and coo-eed. Suzie lifted a limp hand and moved her bag off the next chair. Wankel stared.

'A friend of yours?'

'Sort of.'

To Suzie's own ears it sounded surly so she said, 'I'll introduce you.'

Wankel smiled and said, 'Yes. Please.'

Suzie looked at him sideways, thinking he had somehow swelled up since Miriam's entrance, had puffed out round his shoulders and neck and head like a toad. He did look quite like a toad; Suzie wondered where she could find a china toad in which she could begin to save more pennies; her pig was nearly full. Miriam gushed up and Suzie made the introductions.

'A poet!' little Miri exclaimed opening her eyes wide and looking into Wankel's. 'You are naughty, Suzie! I thought for a minute you said "pervert"!'

Wankel laughed, the first time Suzie had seen him laugh. He had never before allowed himself more than a sardonic smile. He said, indulgently and not without a certain pride, 'Some people would say they're the same thing.'

'Oh, no!' Miriam fluttered a small palm and reaching across Suzie, laid it confidingly on his knee. 'I'm sure no one could ever say that about *you*!'

Wankel looked modest while Suzie looked longingly at the row of lights. Room Four winked on, then straightaway Room Three and Room Five. She stood up and said, 'I must go in.'

Wankel looked up and said, 'Me too.'

And Miriam said, 'And me. Wasn't that quick!'

Wankel was pleasantly surprised at how tall Miriam made him feel, and smiled down at her. 'You're not here for anything serious, I hope?'

'Well! To let you into a secret (I haven't even told my husband yet; dear Herbie!) I think I'm going to be a Mummy again! Isn't it *won*derful?'

Wankel thought what a pleasant change it was to meet a truly feminine woman. Ripe and youthful and. . . . He swallowed hastily for his mouth had begun to water; but a spot of saliva had already crept past his crooked tooth and he had to wipe it furtively off his lip with the back of his hand.

Suzie stopped outside Room Four and Wankel, engrossed in watching the cute sway of Miriam's hips, bumped into her. The contact was unpleasantly angular; it was no wonder he had problems.

The first thing Suzie noticed when she went into Room Four was the noise. It was the kind of noise a hand-mower makes, cutting a country lawn on a summer evening. But this was the middle of winter, the city, and the single window in the room was shut. As she lowered herself hesitantly on to the chair, the doctor removed his forefinger from his nostril and said, 'Ummmm?'

Suzie said, 'I beg your pardon?'

He said again, fingering his stethoscope, 'Ummmm?'

But Suzie did not hear him for the lawnmower, which had

faded as it reached the far end of the lawn, was growing louder again. Suzie looked wildly around the room; it was quite deafening. The stretching feelings multiplied inside her head. She said, 'The mower?'

The doctor said, 'What?'

Suzie yelled, nearly screamed, 'The mower! The mower!'

The doctor reached under the desk and the noise stopped. He said reprovingly, 'There's really no need to shout, you know. This *is* Community Health.'

'But the mower. . . .' said Suzie more quietly. 'Where? What?'

'A – er – little device that most of our patients find relaxing. The sound of a country evening; merely a tape recording; most interesting. I've listened to it hundreds of times and have only just detected the song of the *turdus viscivorus* – the Mistle Thrush, you know. Quite splendid. Now, what seems to be the trouble?'

He put his fingers together in a narrow steeple and leaned forward.

'Well, doctor – er. . . .'

'Alright.'

'Alright?'

'Yes; Alright. My name is Alright.'

'But I thought the other doctor was Alright.'

'Oh, he is.'

'No, his name!'

'That too. We're all Alright. It's one of the principles of Community Health; to inspire confidence in our patients. Now –' he looked down at his wristwatch, 'your five minutes is nearly up; if you could just tell me briefly?'

Suzie swallowed and stared at her hands which were beginning to tremble. 'I – um – I think I'm going mad.'

'Uh-huh.'

'I have these stretching things inside my head.'

'Um.'

'And my mouth keeps growing – you see? See how big it is? Spreading over my face. I've tried to control it, but it's taking over.'

'Mmmm.'

'And I have bad dreams; visions; death; destruction. . . .' Her hands were shaking uncontrollably now; she would have liked to cry, but could not. 'Can you do something, doctor? Can you help me?'

There was a long silence while he looked at her over the precise placing of his finger ends. She heard, quite clearly through the thin partition to her left, a man's voice saying, 'Just a little wider with the thighs!'

And Miriam's girlish giggle as she replied, 'Oooh! It's awfully big and cold!'

And through the partition to her right another man's voice saying, jocular, conspiratorial, 'Can't get it up? Nonsense! One of those thin types – all shoulder, no arse? Women's Libber! Really? Well, get yourself another!'

Suzie rested her head in her hands which, strangely, no longer shook. Across the vast distance from the other side of the desk she heard the chair creak as Doctor Alright leaned back and exhaled a sigh. 'What you need, young lady,' he said, 'is a baby! Next, please.'

5

My poet has become to me rather like a sore that I must cauterize. He lies suppurating on my mind, a crater of disorder which may at any moment spew forth something molten, reducing the normal functions of the brain to ash.

It is, I believe with the as yet untainted sections of my mind, a form of madness. Not for nothing did Van Gogh sever an ear; not for nothing do I anticipate in all its different forms the possible arrival of he who is not yet my lover – that word in itself a misnomer, for I am unaware that the matter has anything to do with love.

It begins in fact to have more to do with the opposite. Not hate precisely, not anything precisely, but a desire to be rid of some debilitating infection; much, perhaps, as Henry VIII felt when the syphilis moved in and claimed him. I have no intention of letting my poet, or my desire for him, claim me. And yet I sense the existence of that fallow field above which quivers the dandelion clock, laden and in need only of a nudge for disaster to occur. Something, I acknowledge, must be done; but the abyss which separates intention from its action is great, and I content myself with looking into it.

Not that I am content. A woman is by nature meant to be content, so legend has it, with husband, home and hearth. I am then unwomanly, a Lil and lusting always for an otherness, that otherness which belongs to men as though by right. And so, my poet; and so the delusions suffered by a million discontented minds which turn the object of desire into something more than human, much less than divine. As if the taking of another to oneself were the answer. One flesh. The ultimate image, packaged like cornflakes; the only way to start your day; never realizing that the one flesh is irrevocably the own.

Other; other; other. The hermit has the right idea perhaps, clasping the self tight in to self, admitting nothing, transmitting nothing, like the oyster clamped around the grain, existence only as the filter, nothing in, nothing out, nothing to change or alter until the revelation and the pearl.

My pearl I shall not cast before swine. My pearl I shall preserve for the descending flies, for records and for vaults, for soft voices chanting outmoded words; tradition; the retrospective promise of continuity.

My poet then, and all that he involves or could involve must be cast out. Were he the devil I could call an exorcist, but he is merely man and I will call upon the exorcist possession who never fails, who drives out demon desire with all the efficacy of a flaming cross. I shall have him, yes, and an ending to the intellectual masturbation that he is; the old equation; one and one makes none.

Then the return to sanity, the regaining of that proportion so beloved of classicists, the ousting of distortion and of dream. Reality, put on like a pair of overalls, within whose protection the uncomfortable persona sweats and strains.

There are times when I would rather not be Lil. When I wish bad men would not come after me, wonder whether all good men are bores. But these times are the few and now must not be one. Like a patient waiting for an operation I prepare myself. Raking the ashes I discover resolution, the product of many fires. My poet: you do not know; you do not know.

Oh Lil; I wonder whether you will give your poet up? You have lied to me so often, I can no longer trust the things you say. But why must you insist on lying while I insist on truth? Our life together would be so much simpler if we could agree on this one point.

But the trouble is with truth it is often inconvenient; it cannot be cast out at every whim, put aside and forgotten like a shoe which pinches; and you will not be inconvenienced. So you lie as easily and pleasantly as you tell the truth, it is merely a question of circumstance. To you a lie is like the brief eclipsing of the sun behind a summer cloud, a temporary and insignificant cooling of the temperature.

Why have you never understood that it is not like that? That lies are never told in isolation? They build up one on to the other like bricks in the construction of a house; they seem individually perfect, collectively a perfect edifice. But inside it is sub-standard, full of cracks, weak, crumbling and soft centred.

Your house of lies you now inhabit with your poet; for how else are such affairs to be conducted? You must say you are where you are not, and you are not where you are; that you have seen this one or that one, have said these words, felt this emotion, not felt that. Until the lies take on a separate truth themselves, the false world becomes real, the balance of things is lost.

Because I speak the truth my sense of balance is secure; I know what is reality. But what is yours? Sometimes it changes so rapidly, like sunlight over a fresh sea, that I am afraid for you. As for one who has stepped from the high ledge into the temporary freedom of the air and twists leaf-light, down through the limbo of her own brief measuring.

Wankel was standing naked looking at his reflection in the mirror. It was a particularly good quality mirror, fronting as it did his favourite piece of furniture, an Edwardian oak wardrobe, given to him by an ex-wife.

But tonight he wished that the mirror's quality was not so good, wished the reflection of his image was less true and clear. For under the inadequate shading of the overhead electric light, each imperfection of his body, each blemish marring the surface of his skin, seemed magnified, so that his whole self appeared to be composed of imperfections. He lifted his chin in an effort to dispel a wattle of flesh which had spawned since his last inspection, and hung like a flaccid tyre below his jaw bone. He tightened his facial muscles, composed them into an appealing look; the image in the mirror leered horribly back at him. He said, 'Fuck it!' and the Wankel image raised its eyebrows in silent reproof.

It was Christmas Eve and he was waiting for Suzie to arrive.

He had almost decided this would be the last time. He had taken Doctor Alright's advice seriously, as one man should take another's. For if you could not trust your own kind, and a professional at that, what hope was there?

He thought, for himself and Suzie, there was little. And she had really seemed so plain in comparison to Miriam. He should find one like Miriam; his second wife had been a little like her; he wondered why he had ever let her go.

He hesitated in front of the mirror, wanting to get dressed, for the room was rather cold and goose pimples were beginning to erupt along his arm and inner thigh; but at the same time wanting – he did not know quite what. He looked at his reflection in the mirror once again, seeing this time a shadow of the Wankel-image of his dream, lit against the darkness, moving to the roar of many throats. Then the image faded and he saw no more than his imperfect self, and sighed. But the idea remained and drew him from the mirror to a chest of drawers, where he paused, before reaching in the topmost drawer and pulling out a handful of ladies' underwear. Not the delicious, tiny, frothy, feminine kind of thing he had acquired for Suzie; no, these that he now held and fondled resembled more a suit of female armour, whalebone and calico, and were besides heavy and large. He lifted to his nose a stiff suspender belt, given a forbidding shape of its own by the wealth of bone and padding such as might prop up a sagging building, a totally fallen female gut, and inhaled the pleasant perfume of mothballs and must. His mother's, taken secretly out of her attic trunk the day before, when he had visited her on the pretext of taking nothing more than tea. And ever since his secret longing had been to try them on, to feel the woman-cloth against his own skin. This longing had gone nearly unacknowledged, kept as it was just below the surface of his mind, like a submarine going gently forward, causing barely a ripple, armed with the means of destruction.

But now with the shudder of it passing almost painfully through him, he whispered to himself, 'I want; I want. . . .'

But holding the taboo material against him, rubbing the

forbidden fibres over chest, belly and thigh, still something prevented him.

'If only,' he thought, and knew at once the answer. Suzie. He folded the edges of the things together carefully (for he had a tidy mind) and put them carefully away.

He got dressed, applying a liberal helping of scented powder. He combed his hair. All so careful, so calm, controlled as the waters held at a lock, waiting only for the gates to be lifted.

If only she would come! Where before he had thought of Suzie's arrival with something close to indifference, now he waited for it eagerly, wishing the intervening time away. Not even 'Bolshevik Love Poetry' could claim superior attraction. He did not even want to hear his Bach. He sat, in the quiet room, his hands folded loosely across his trousered thigh, and thought of nothing, while the sounds of feast and celebration grew outside his window, and across the street a plastic angel hanging in a naked window swayed and swung.

A banner spanning the width of Rookum's doorway proclaimed Christ the King. Suzie, battling her way through the Christmas crowd, doubted it. She was nervously behind time, worried she would be late for Wankel. She clutched against her chest, for once glad it was rather flat, a record, Bach, a present for him, one she hoped he did not have.

An hour's indecision, fluttering above the record racks like a homeless butterfly, had put her behind. Then another half before the mirror in the ladies' lavatory, trying to repair the ravages thirty-three years had worked upon her face. She wanted to look her best; she wanted to be wanted. She had put on a skirt, narrow at the knees, and a pair of shoes with silly, thin heels. She had already turned her ankle on the escalator; perhaps it was a sign.

Coming out of Rookum's she stumbled on a broken pavement slab and fell into a crowd of drunken office workers singing 'Silent Night'.

She did not like Christmas. She did not like excess of any kind.

Christmas had become an orgiastic gorging of food and fun. And the fun did not even seem like fun; it seemed to Suzie rather like hard work. Her mind recoiled from the thought of work, more specifically unfinished work, her article, not even limping along, its presence behind her curtained desk like a laid-out corpse, waiting to be carried away.

She shuddered, hurrying past the brightly-lit shop windows, garish scenes, balloons and babes, trumpery, tinsel, swelling turkeys, hampers overflowing with the best there was. The air reeked of booze and *bonhomie*. Suzie could not feel part of it. And when she thankfully turned out of the wider streets into the narrower, darker sideroads, still the feeling of separateness remained. She thought once that she caught sight of Rex, crossing in front of her, passing under an orange lamp which licked small tongues of flame over the surface of his head and neck. But it could not be him for she had left him in his room. And she was beginning to disbelieve the thoughts she had of him before, his spying, his always home before her. She was beginning to believe that perhaps she was a little mad. And strangely the thought disturbed her less and less. Madness was just another way of being; you could not help it, you were the way you were. Except, she could not be the way she was with Wankel. Tonight she was trying to be as he would have her be, she was even wearing stockings and was conscious of an uncomfortable draught around the upper reaches of her thighs. She tried to press her legs more closely together but it did not help. At the same time she remembered to hold in her mouth. This morning she had noticed some further growth and was becoming increasingly disturbed; but she did not want to think about that now. She wanted Wankel, was on her way to him, would have him; would have him.

And as she walked she avoided looking at the buildings, ignored the city, kept her eyes on the smallest area of pavement it was possible to see, just in front of her, in case she fell. She would have preferred to be blindfold, but that was impractical. For she wanted no sense of threat or ruin to enter her tonight.

But although she did not look she was uncomfortably aware

of everything she passed, old houses, new, of brick, of concrete, stone walls and railings, windows, wood. And from it all she felt a strangeness ooze out and descend around her like settling mist; she could almost have sworn there was a mist, a layer of something between her and all that surrounded her, a membrane of alienation. And the city here seemed unnaturally quiet, like a churchyard no one visits any more, whose stones will soon be taken up and planted in old vaults. She thought, 'I am afraid,' in the way she sometimes did when she was wholly alone, though now she was not alone, small groups of people hung about the corners kicking stones. They frightened her, their warding off the cold with no more than a hunched-in shoulder, warding off her presence with a look.

It did not seem like Christmas here; it seemed like any brooding of boredom and discontent. At last through Lazarus Street, deserted, more silent even than the rest, past the obscene graffiti scrawled beneath the naked feet of Christ, on to the house where Wankel had his rooms, the accelerated heartbeat, the nervous knuckle calling him towards the door.

She thought, in the uncertain lighting, why, he looks quite young! and almost despite himself he thought, Suzie! Ah, Suzie! Really, a remarkable woman for thirty-three. And a skirt! And those delicious little shoes! Perhaps it was a sign; perhaps this was the night.

He drew her in, took her jacket from her as a gentleman should, tried not to eye too openly her breasts, very visible under a clinging shirt. He was determined this evening on all those little observances which make life civilized, distinguish man from man, impart to woman those extra elements of femininity. He kissed her cold fingers and offered her a drink. She stopped herself just in time from snatching back her hand, the touch of his lips on her skin rubbery and damp, and accepted a gin. Wankel nudged his full glass against hers and said, 'Here's to us!' looking meaningfully into her eyes. And she mouthed the dutiful echo, 'Here's to us!'

Bach boomed as if in approbation. Wankel had put on one of his favourites, convinced there was nothing like a little background music. He said, 'Ah, the Brandenburg! Incomparable!'

Suzie put down her drink and picked up her gift-wrapped record and said, 'Um; Happy Christmas.'

'For me?'

Suzie thought, he really does look quite young when he smiles. Tonight he looks younger altogether; what can it be? His hair; it seems less grey; I wonder. . . .

'For you.'

Wankel took the parcel from her, relieved that she had ceased looking at his head. He had that morning made a judicious application of that liquid guaranteed to take ten years off any man. He hoped he had not overdone it; he did not want to be thought effete. The inner wrapping fell away and Wankel said, 'How wonderful! A record! I love records.' Then, 'Well! The Brandenburg! How, er –'

'You can always change it; they said if it was wrong you could change it.'

'Change it!' He hugged the coloured sleeve into his chest as though someone had attempted to take it from him by force. 'I couldn't do *that*!'

Suzie looked at him rather surprised over the rim of her nearly empty glass and was about to ask why not, but saw in time how charged his eyebrows were with significance. She changed her query to a simper and held out her glass for more. As he took it from her he squeezed her fingers gently, knowingly.

'Wouldn't you be more comfortable sitting down?'

'Er, yes,' said Suzie, pushing her glasses high up on her nose. 'I suppose I would.'

And then began the sequence of events, the pattern of thought and action, word and look which, while to the disinterested observer may have all the hallmarks of a badly acted panto-mime, to the participants is of the highest interest and import-ance, being the accepted prelude to the evening's entertain-ment. In short, there are certain formalities to be observed before a fuck.

And so, the little endearments accompanied increasingly by breathy sighs; the squeeze here; the tentative more intimate fondle there; the – is that more comfortable? the – shall I? would you mind? the ohs, the ahs, the half-closed eyes, the salivated kisses.

To their mutual surprise, Wankel found Suzie naked and Suzie found Wankel in the nude. They each paused briefly and surveyed the other, but not too closely, as Wankel had luckily turned down the lights. Then he said, 'Ah, Suzie!' And she said, 'Ah, Wankel!' and the affair began in earnest.

And rather like gourmet diners who have stimulated their appetites with a variety of tasty hors d'oeuvres, and do not want to be full up before all courses have been tried, Wankel and Suzie approached their main dish circumspectly.

Wankel, whose appetite seemed in no danger of flagging, was helping his digestion with visions of Miriam, voluptuous and lying in his arms, Miriam in lace and lycra, Miriam whose suspender he now playfully tweaked, relishing the snapping sound it made recoiling back against her skin. Suzie's small 'ow!' did spoil things that little bit, but he shut his eyes more tightly and refused to be disturbed.

And Suzie was thinking how pleasant all this was, her Wankel hers at last. She desired for her own imperfect self, everything just right, or as right as it was possible for things to be. She contemplated, as is usual with women at these special moments, those things that were important to her; sex and intellect. My article, she thought, and in the glow of mounting passion it did seem to her that not only might she finish it, soon, tomorrow, but it would surely make her fortune, send her on the road to scholarship and fame, guest speaker, someday, at a literary luncheon.

'I love your things.'

Suzie eased one hip a little to the right, feeling like a ridden horse. 'Um.'

She smiled; it was so nice to be appreciated for oneself.

'No, really; black is my favourite colour.'

She opened one eye. Her things; those things; she had forgotten she had them on; the stupid uniform she had worn just to please him; she wished he had forgotten too; she felt hurt.

'You look lovely.'

She sighed; that was more acceptable; perhaps he would be quiet now, and she could think her own thoughts again. But he said, 'Suzie. . . .'

She made vague noises, wishing he would just go on, go on.

'I'd, er, like to, too.'

'Like to what?' she muttered vaguely. 'Do; do.'

'You're sure you won't mind? It won't upset you?'

'Nah, nah.'

'I really can?'

'Ya, ya.'

If only he would get on with whatever it was. It could not be anything too awful; he was not the type. She was rather surprised when he leapt up suddenly agile and began rummaging in the chest of drawers. He said, 'Don't look.'

She began to be alarmed, but her sense of fair play would not allow her to peep. Soon she felt his weight again and was relieved to discover nothing obvious, no whips or spurs, no rubber wet suit, snorkel, mask. She said, 'What –' but then as she placed her two hands on his ample buttocks (their position being missionary) she found instead of flesh a wealth of whalebone, and further down, the smoothness of stocking encasing a hairy thigh. He said, through thick lips, 'You don't know what this means to me.'

And Suzie said, 'I do. I do.'

The record had come to an end and the room was silent except for the rhythmic squeaking of sofa springs, the creaking of whalebone. Suzie stared at a crack in the ceiling thinking how badly it needed a coat of paint. Outside the window in the quiet street, there was a sudden shuffle of feet and the ringing of the doorbell, heralding the chant 'O Come All Ye Faithful'. Wankel made a mewing sound like a hurt kitten. The chorus of voices swelled outside the door, 'O come ye, O COME ye. . . .' Wankel propped himself up on one elbow, beads of sweat sprouting greyly on his forehead. He looked, thought Suzie, like a half-drowned dog, as despairing. The chorus petered out ragged and uncertain into a heavy silence.

Then Suzie heard from not far off a scream, an ugly scream which pierced through street, window, wall; and then more screams and the sudden sound of many feet, yells, curses, an explosion, and the orange light cast by the bursting into life of flame. Somebody shouted, 'Riot! Police!' but the voice was drowned out by the sound of breaking glass and falling brick.

'What?' said Wankel.

'Oh my God,' said Suzie.

And then Suzie saw in slow motion, like the running down of a reel of film, the curtain at Wankel's window billow inwards, full skirt on a blustery day, and behind it, just behind it, the window coming in.

They half fell off the sofa, separate now as if they had never been otherwise, lust forgotten, Suzie stumbling over the brick which flowered surrealistically upon the carpet, Wankel bulging ridiculously above and below the calico, soft belly, soft thigh. They stared at the ruin of the window then at each other.

Wankel said, 'The Revolution!'

Suzie said, 'My knickers!'

Hurriedly, fumblingly, they got dressed, not looking at each other, listening to the sounds which swelled and faded, sometimes near, sometimes so faint as to be hardly distinguishable, the sirens and the urgent bells, the clang of a fire engine, motors revving, and below it all, the bubbling like a phlegm-filled chest of violence and discontent.

Wankel grabbed his coat, making sure his notebook and two pens were in the pocket. The Glorious Revolution! A poem could easily come out of this. He was determined to be prepared. He put his two hands on Suzie's shoulders, kissed her once on each pale cheek, lengthened his short neck and said, 'My Mother!'

Suzie buttoned her jacket, pushed her glasses high up on her nose and said, 'My green front door!'

They stared steadfastly at each other.

'Duty!'

'Duty!'

On the pavement they stopped and looked at each other again. Wankel said, 'It's been nice.'

Suzie said, 'Hasn't it.'

They both said, 'When this is over. . . .'

They clasped hands briefly then Wankel turned up his coat collar and went left, Suzie adjusted her glasses and went right. Wankel began to hum 'We'll Meet Again'; Suzie, on the point of la-la-ing 'The White Cliffs of Dover', saw a shadow in a doorway which had the shape of Rex, and broke into an ungainly run.

In the empty room where Suzie's Wankel lived, a Christmas card, caught by the draught from the shattered window, tipped from the mantelpiece and fluttered to the carpet where it lay with the broken glass, the brick. On it was written in gold, 'Across the Miles'; and in black ink, 'With Love From Mother. P. S. Are You Comin' Home fer Christmas, Son?'

Wankel thought there was not much to it until he came to Lazarus Street. There he found something resembling the visions of Hell beloved of the Old Masters. Dodging through darkened alleys he had managed to avoid the riot, or as it was in his mind, the revolution. A fugitive or two had cantered past him chanting stirring slogans and there was an acceptable amount of looting going on. He had witnessed one rape and felt a little sorry for the girl; but it was all part of the class war, and she was probably a prostitute.

But going to his mother's house – not without a twinge of party conscience that he was putting family first – he had to pass close to the end of Lazarus Street, and as he neared it he was drawn into the edges of the crowd which yelled and milled among the buildings there. And then he had no choice but to continue on with them as they formed into ragged ranks and charged the helmeted and shielded line of police, past upturned blazing cars, past pools of flame formed from petrol bombs.

Wankel was afraid, but at the same time, elated. A strange euphoria overtook him so that as the mob roared he roared too, as the citizen next to him picked up a brick so did he, and they hurled and howled in unison. And what a poem this would make! An epic! Why, he might even branch out, try his hand at a novel. For tonight he was capable of anything, he was Wankel incarnate, Wankel divine.

The line of helmets was retreating; someone screamed, 'The church!'

The crowd, as if with a single will, stopped and looked up at the dark shape of the church from which began to bloom light after light until the whole was filled with light, until it seemed St Lazarus' Church was the new seat of some misplaced sun. In front of it a Christmas tree leaned drunkenly, its own small lights still on, pale and puny.

A figure came out onto the parapet beside the broken window and the severed feet of Christ. It had long hair which flowed onto its shoulders, some long garment flowing out about the legs, reminiscent of an ancient robe. It paused, a silhouette of darkness cut out from the background light; and very clearly Wankel saw its arm curve forward in a slow arc, from its hand like a wingless bird came something which alighted in the front rank of the mob, a plume of fire. And then another, and another from the same arcing arm and screams, cries, 'Not us, not us!'; the breaking and running, the blue-clad figures rushing the front door of the church. And over it all, from the parapet, the unholy shrieks and chuckles of glee, as the arm arced, arm arced. . . .

Wankel thought, it can't be!

But at that moment one of the objects fell quite close to him, its blast singeing the edges of his coat. He staggered as best he could into the protection of a wall. He felt dizzy, could hardly see. Across the street someone whose clothes were alight screamed horribly. And from the parapet a longer, higher scream, a burst of flame, then silence.

Wankel shook his head to try and clear it; the euphoria had wholly gone. He felt rather sick, and decided the excitement was not good for him. The street was quieter now, people shuffling away, order and ambulances coming in again. From the doorway of the church two policemen were carrying a figure in a long robe. Its hair hung loose and witch-like, brushing the top step as they came awkwardly down. Wankel looked and thought again, it can't be.

But as they came close to him he saw it was. He said, 'Mother!'

Wankel's mother lifted her head and, raising two bloody stumps where once her Scrabble-winning hands had been, smiled at him fondly and said, 'Don't you worry about me, Son. Don't you worry about your mother.'

When Suzie got to her own street it was deserted. It seemed to be quite unaffected, street lights on and whole, Christmas trees glowing in windows, net curtains firmly hung.

Suzie was very relieved. She had run most of the way from Wankel's rooms and her feet, in their silly shoes, hurt badly. She wished, for the twentieth time, that she had worn some others. She had even tried taking them off, but the pavement, though it seemed so smooth, in reality had hundreds of little sharp edged stones, all waiting for the placement of Suzie's delicate sole.

As she limped towards the green front door she acknowledged there were more momentous things tonight than her sore feet. But despite what anybody said, sore feet did matter; sore feet affected everything. How could you get on with a revolution when every step produced a little dart of pain which collected somewhere in the region of your ankle bone and throbbed there, causing you to think of nothing but mustard bowls and bath salts. Look at her – not taking part in any revolution it is true, but hurrying home to fight a rearguard action, if the need arose, in defence of her own property, husband, home and hearth.

Suzie broke into a stumbling run as she reached the iron railings marking her territory's edge. She felt a peculiar feeling, and wondered if it might be joy. My green front door! My through-lounge! All safe, untouched as the possessions of the righteous should always be. She fumbled in her handbag for the key.

From the corner of the street she heard a victorious whoop, a wail of blood-lust or delight, the tramp of booted feet. Into view at a dead run, weapons at the ready, came a regiment of women, bayonets formed of broomsticks, each one tipped by a burning bra, whose flame-enveloped cups jiggled to the chorus 'WAG for Women!'. Suzie saw at a glance it was the WAG executive, her nightmare here, reality at last. She fumbled for the key, her heavy fingers losing it among the debris at the bottom of her bag. She battered frantically upon her own front door, pressed her three-chime bell again and again, cried, 'Help! Help! Let me in!

Above her a curtain twitched and she could see her lodger's face pressed up against the glass. Rex. Always home before her. Always home.

The chairperson was nearly up to her, terrible in khaki, and with khaki-coloured eyes. Suzie said, 'Wait! Oh, please, I can explain; it's nearly –'

But they moved in on her, silent now and huge as she sank down on her knees, their eyes an accusation which she nearly understood before the smoke from smouldering cups overcame her and she fell insensible onto the step.

6

Larry was sitting in his overcoat in a deckchair on the sand. The beach was deserted, he supposed because it was a little cold. January was not a favourite time for sea and sand. Beside him were his newspapers folded in a neat pile to avoid being ruffled by the wind, and held down by a rock. His quota for the day was nearly done. That pleasant feeling of a job nearly completed, food for the inner man, was beginning to warm through him. He wondered idly where Suzie was, but the thought was no more than a sliver pared accidentally from the carved symmetry of his mind, immediately lost.

A gull flying over the beach just then might have cast a curious eye at his dark speck, interruption of the smoothness of the shore, a clothed incongruity marring the naked stretch of sand.

And going further, over the water and the white-tipped waves, beyond where the tide clasps the cold rock, out above the wider, smoother sea, such gull might have perceived another speck, paler, less substance to it, floating out and floating out, Suzie, swimming a grey, cold ocean. Suzie, to whom her Wankel is no more now than the silver fish which nudges at her knee; whose arms, as she swims slowly on, cause small ripples which break the surface of the water like little wounds; until gradually the ripples break more slowly, fade away, and all the wounds heal over, and the sea is smooth again and whole.

What can be done with Wankel? Or the wider question, what *does* one do with a poet?

He could be left, perhaps, kneeling at his mother's empty urn

147

(for her wounds did prove fatal), heart broken. But a poet's heart is far more resilient than that.

It was three o'clock. Wankel was walking down Lazarus Street, stepping carefully over the piles of rubble which still stood there, keeping a safe distance from the scarred walls of the ruins that remained. He paused as the church clock sounded the hour close above his head. He wondered vaguely whether it might not be some kind of sign; but so many things were happening nowadays, you could no longer tell.

He stopped by the little iron gate through which he and Suzie had come out that day of the fallen Christ, and felt rather glum. Suzie! What times they had had! Really, a remarkable woman for thirty-three. He sighed. The gravestones rose before him dark and whole, they alone undamaged, even the concrete angel still lifting an admonitory hand. He felt a little thrill, that familiar twinge, that stirring which says a poem is coming on. The title took him by surprise, its power, its originality, 'Elegy'. He smiled widely, forgetting his crooked tooth, 'Elegy for Suzie'.

He reached in his pocket for his notebook, but saw it had begun to rain; his hands would get wet, the book too; it could wait until he got home. He turned up his coat collar and walked on again, a single figure growing smaller down the ruined street. As he turned the corner he began to hum, no more than a small vibration in the back of his throat.

Could May be having an affair with Larry? Maybe. Maybe not. I have been watching them closely for several days, and have detected nothing. Perhaps it is what passes for my conscience speaking from some hidden depth. For I am planning consummation.

The day is not conducive to such a plan. I do not believe in the pathetic fallacy, but it is pleasant to have sun and sky as backcloth to the present, nearer prospect of desire gratified. I must do without.

For it has been a hellish week; the sort of week in January which swears spring will never come; when the sky crouches so low over the city that the tower blocks reach up and pierce the swelling of its gut, and you imagine it must soon rain blood.

My mood, as I go to meet my poet, is melancholy. It is our third attempt. First he ailed with influenza; then there were floods, a bridge swept away, a woman drowned. I wonder, is it an omen, then dismiss the thought as an extravagance. I have little time for omens, flights of fancy and the like.

My poet has chosen an inconvenient spot. More than an hour from the city, a little out-of-the-way hotel which once did duty for a genteel horde of country-bred Edwardians. I can see them now, in bodices of striped organza, swaying over their mallets on the croquet lawn.

But many weeds have sprouted in the crevices between the paving stones since then. Weeds greet me as I turn the car into the drive; weeds sway in from the untrimmed hedges as the car sweeps past; and there are weeds pushing their way up through the gravel of the empty courtyard as I walk towards the wide stone steps, wide as a waiting mouth.

To go in is to become another world. I do not believe the woman at the desk is real. She seems carved from the same oak as counter, floor, staircase, panelling. The hallway (for it cannot disguise itself as a hotel foyer) is in feeling like an oaken box. To close the outside door behind me is to step in and pull down the lid.

And perhaps it is Pandora's box, for here complexions alter. My poet, they tell me, has not yet arrived. I wonder, idly, if he will ever come, for I have ceased to care.

And poets, as I carry my small case up the wide stairs, have come to seem – I do not know how it can be – irrelevant; my poet in particular rather ineffectual and effete. I imagine him with difficulty and discover he is short, though I had previously supposed him tall. I am surprised by it. I have always preferred men of stature, men of muscle and solidity.

The room is on the top floor of the house, as far away as it is possible to be; and all the rooms are empty, except mine. There is no one but the woman in the hall who sits, to my altered imagination, like Charon guarding the river Styx.

The walls of the room are covered in tiny flowers whose dark stems twine and interlink. I could imagine, if I had freed my mind sufficiently, that I was in a secret place composed entirely of flowers, like the one which as a small girl, I could crawl inside to dream.

This room, my presence here, is rather dreamlike. I take out my things and hang them up in careful slow motion, handling for longer than the others a wrapper of white silk which I have bought to honour the occasion. Such whimsicality would irritate me if I were not so calm, my mind a sea whose vast inertia no wind can ruffle. I place the wrapper on the bed and study it.

How many women have searched the symbols of themselves as I do, seeking the answer to a question hardly formed, hoping from a fragment to construct the whole, courting completion? Perhaps in desiring my poet I desire no more than myself. If he should come, if he should not come, still, the wrapper, the room, the mind, the me.

It is so quiet here; I feel that I could open any door and let a deeper silence in. But I sit down on the bed, lie down, lie across the wide bed as though it were some shore and I prostrate, willing the sea-god. I do not sleep but wait and wait in this curious limbo; perhaps an hour has passed, I can no longer tell; this room is the still centre at the eye of time.

And then without my hearing him my poet, around whom the air eddies gently; rather, I believe it to be him, there is no telling here, where the petals on the walls are losing their identity to an early dusk, night flowers, drained of colour, scentless and stiff. So my poet, formless as a new moon; and yet, the he, the I, the hand, the lip; and it begins to be in the way that these things sometimes are, quite good.

But as his hand touches my thigh I see it is no more than the hand of any ghost, bone only, or the mirage of bone, a jointed claw. From somewhere I can here him say my name. 'Lilian,' he says, and 'Lilian?' as though he did not understand me. Yet he must know that I am Lilian, white flower held in a white hand, each cell untouched and pure, yes, pure though my flesh falls putrefying into the grave of my death.